KRISTY IN CHARGE

**Other books by
Ann M. Martin**

P.S. Longer Letter Later (written with Paula Danziger)
Leo the Magnificat
Rachel Parker, Kindergarten Show-off
Eleven Kids, One Summer
Ma and Pa Dracula
Yours Turly, Shirley
Ten Kids, No Pets
Slam Book
Just a Summer Romance
Missing Since Monday
With You and Without You
Me and Katie (the Pest)
Stage Fright
Inside Out
Bummer Summer

THE KIDS IN MS. COLMAN'S CLASS series
BABY-SITTERS LITTLE SISTER series
THE BABY-SITTERS CLUB mysteries
THE BABY-SITTERS CLUB series
CALIFORNIA DIARIES series

KRISTY IN CHARGE

Ann M. Martin

AN
APPLE
PAPERBACK

SCHOLASTIC INC.
New York Toronto London Auckland Sydney

Cover art by Hodges Soileau

ISBN 0-590-50064-3

12 11 10 9 8 7 6 5 4 3 2 1   8 9/9 0 1 2 3/0

Printed in the U.S.A.   40
First Scholastic printing, September 1998

The author gratefully acknowledges
Suzanne Weyn
for her help in
preparing this manuscript.

CHAPTER 1

I sat forward at my desk and gave Ms. Garcia my complete attention. She's my homeroom teacher, and what she was telling our class this morning was extremely interesting to me.

"This year the Stoneybrook Board of Education has worked with other schools in southern Connecticut and has come up with a new program called TOT — Teachers of Tomorrow. For three days student volunteers will be teaching some classes in place of the teachers," she told us.

Yess! I thought. My friends call me Kristy Thomas, the Idea Machine, and I guess the name fits. Instantly, I was thinking of a million ways Stoneybrook Middle School (otherwise known as SMS) could be improved.

I raised my hand. "Yes, Kristy?" Ms. Garcia said.

"Is Mr. Taylor's job available?"

"You want to be the principal?" Ms. Garcia asked with a smile.

The class laughed. I was slightly embarrassed, but I just grinned and shrugged.

What's wrong with wanting to be in charge? I couldn't think of anyone else in the eighth grade better equipped for the job. After all, I *have* experience in running things. I formed a softball team for little kids called Kristy's Krushers. And I'm founder and president of the Baby-sitters Club. I'll tell you more about that later, but for now let me say that the BSC (as we call it) is more than a club. It's a very successful business.

"I don't think the principal's job is open," Ms. Garcia said. "But let me tell you how this is going to work."

Ms. Garcia went on to explain that any kid who was interested could volunteer to student teach. That would involve teaching in another class every other day for a week (three times total). We'd have to go through a teacher training course and submit prepared lesson plans, just like a real teacher does.

A troubling thought hit me. Did I look enough like a teacher to control a class of SMS kids? For one thing, I'm only five feet tall, which makes me the smallest kid in my grade. And I don't look particularly sophisticated. No makeup. No jewelry. I wear my long brown hair plain and like no-fuss clothes such as jeans, sweatshirts, and sweaters.

Naw, not a problem, I decided. Although I had never taken the place of an adult, I'd never, ever had trouble leading a group.

"You'll get to experience what we teachers go through," Ms. Garcia continued. "Also, we hope some of you will be inspired to become teachers yourselves someday."

A girl named Cokie Mason (whom I can't stand because she's mean, conceited, and generally obnoxious) appeared at the door with some papers to give Ms. Garcia. She'd stood there long enough to hear what Ms. Garcia had been saying. "Will TOT volunteers be dismissed from their regular classes those days?" she asked as she handed Ms. Garcia the stack of papers.

Well, duh. Cokie has never been a bright light, but this was a dumb question even for her. Did she really think she'd be expected to be in two places at once?

"You'll attend your regular classes except for the class periods when you are teaching another class," Ms. Garcia explained.

"Cool!" Cokie said with a giggle as she left the room.

I couldn't imagine being in a class taught by Cokie. I raised my hand and asked, "Can anybody do this?"

Ms. Garcia nodded. "As long as you take the training course. Also, I should mention, those students who do volunteer will receive extra credit for their work."

I was definitely going to volunteer. Even if I couldn't be principal, I had ideas about how some of my classes could be improved. For example, Ms. Griswold, my science teacher, tends to ignore a bunch of goof-off boys who sit in the back of the class. I'd make them work or get out. They distract everyone who sits near them. And Mrs. Simon, my English teacher, although she's very nice, picks the dullest things for us to read. I'd assign books that are much more enjoyable.

I wondered which class I'd be assigned to. I was eager to know so I could start planning my lessons right away.

It was time to move on to my first period class. Before I left homeroom, I spoke to Ms. Garcia. "I'd like to volunteer," I told her.

"You'll have to wait until Monday," she replied. "We want to give students the weekend to think it over. We only want kids who are serious and who can give the project the time it requires."

"That makes sense," I agreed. "All right. I'll sign up then."

Outside in the crowded hall I saw my friend (and neighbor) Abby Stevenson hurrying to class. "Hey, Abby!" I called to her.

She turned and waited for me. "Hi," she said. "What's up?"

"This student teaching thing is going to be awesome, isn't it?" I said as we began walking together down the hall.

"Are you going to do that?" she cried. "Why would you? It's so much extra work!"

"It's also extra credit," I reminded her.

"You get great grades. You don't need extra credit. You just want to boss kids around."

And my friends say *I'm* too blunt.

"No, I don't!" I objected. (Though I secretly wondered if there was a grain of truth to her comment.) A grin slowly spread across my face. "I want to boss the *teachers* around."

"Oh, way to go," Abby said with a laugh. "How do you expect to do *that*?"

"I want to show them how they've been messing up in their classes. Show by example, I mean."

Abby rolled her eyes. "I don't know. It sounds like too much work to me. Do you still want me to come over tonight?"

"Yeah," I said. "I'd love the company — and the help. David Michael and Karen don't act as goofy when someone not related to them is there."

That night I was sitting for my baby sister, Emily Michelle, who is two and a half;

my younger brother, David Michael (who is seven), and my stepsister, Karen (also seven). I also have two older brothers, Sam (fifteen) and Charlie (seventeen), and a stepbrother, Andrew (five), who is staying with his mother in Chicago for a few months.

It sounds like a full house, doesn't it? It's even more full. My grandmother, Nannie, lives with us. And we have a Bernese mountain dog puppy named Shannon, a fat old cat named Boo-Boo, and several other pets, including a puppy we are training to be a guide dog.

Luckily, it's a big house. A mansion, to be exact. Nine bedrooms and three floors! (The top floor is the attic.) It took a little getting used to at first. You see, we (Mom, my brothers, and I) started out living in a pretty average house. Our dad left us right after David Michael was born (which is all I'll say about him). Mom somehow managed to keep everything together. Then she married Watson Brewer and we all moved across town into the mansion.

"David Michael and Karen are fun," Abby objected. "And Emily Michelle is a doll!"

I smiled. They really *are* great kids. But having Abby around for backup was still a good idea.

Ahead of me I saw Alan Gray. Some kids call

him the class clown. I'd vote him Most Obnoxious.

"The lunatics are about to take over the asy-
lum!" he shouted.

"Do you really want *him* as your teacher?"
Abby asked, jerking her thumb in Alan's direction.

Alan whirled around to face us. "I'd be a
great teacher. We'd study comic books. And
rock lyrics. The things that really matter in this
world."

"Fabulous, Alan," Abby said dryly. "See
what I mean?" she said after he was gone.
"This idea has major drawbacks, if you ask
me."

As it turned out, she was right. The idea had
more drawbacks than either of us could ever
have imagined.

"**W**ho's doing TOT?" Stacey McGill asked that afternoon before our Friday BSC meeting. We were in Claudia Kishi's bedroom, where we hold meetings.

"I'd love to do it," Stacey continued, "if I could be sure I'd get a math class." Stacey is a math whiz and the club treasurer.

"You can't pick," Mallory Pike told her. "I already asked. You have to take the class the TOT coordinator assigns you."

Claudia ripped open a bag of popcorn. "There's no way I'm doing it," she said firmly. That was no surprise. School is not one of her favorite things. She'd probably rather go to the dentist than go to school.

Glancing at the clock, I saw it was five-thirty. Time to start the meeting. I checked the room. Everyone was there. *Good*, I thought. It really bugs me when anyone comes late. "This BSC meeting is about to begin," I announced.

As I mentioned earlier, I came up with the idea for the BSC. One day when I was in seventh grade, my mother spent hours calling around for a sitter for David Michael. That's when the idea came to me. If she could call one number and talk to lots of sitters, she'd probably call that number every time she needed a baby-sitter. For her, it would be easy and wonderful.

And for me — it would be a great business.

So I talked to my best friend and neighbor, Mary Anne Spier, and then to Claudia and Stacey. We agreed to meet in Claudia's room since she has her own phone line. Then we let parents know they could reach us on Monday, Wednesday, and Friday afternoons from five-thirty until six at Claudia's number.

We were an instant success! We had so much work that we brought Dawn Schafer into the club. Later, when Stacey had to move, we added Mallory and Jessica Ramsey. When Stacey returned to Stoneybrook it was no problem because our client list had grown so much that we needed even more help. Then Dawn moved back to California, where she'd grown up, and we had to replace her. Enter: Abby. That makes ten members right now. (Seven regulars, two associates, and one honorary, since Dawn visits fairly often and always comes to meetings when she's here.)

The phone rang. Claudia scooped up the receiver. "Hello, Baby-sitters Club," she answered. Listening carefully, she took the client's information down on a pad, then said she'd call right back. She turned to Mallory. "It was your mom. She wants someone for this Thursday, but just for Vanessa, Margo, and Claire." Mallory is one of eight kids. Sitting for only three of them is a breeze compared to dealing with the whole crew.

"Yeah, I can't do it Thursday," Mallory explained. "TOT training. I asked ahead to make sure I'd be available."

"Then a lot of us can't take the job," Mary Anne said as she opened the BSC record book where, as club secretary, she keeps track of all our jobs. "I wanted to volunteer too." She looked at Claudia. "You said you didn't want to do it, right?"

"Me? No way," Claudia replied. "I'm definitely free for Thursday."

"I'm not doing TOT," Jessi said. "But I can't sit either. I just started an extra ballet class on Thursdays."

"I'm not doing TOT either," Abby added.

Mary Anne looked down at her book. "But you have an allergist appointment that day," she reminded Abby.

Mary Anne not only records all our jobs in the record book, she also keeps track of our appointments and after-school activities, so there's never a conflict. She's awesome at it.

"I'll go," Claudia said as she punched in the Pikes' phone number to tell Mrs. Pike she was coming on Thursday.

"The training is on Friday too," Mallory mentioned to Mary Anne. "I won't be available on that day either."

"I'd better find out now who's going to TOT training and who isn't, so I can schedule everyone properly," Mary Anne proposed. "Everyone who *is* going, raise your hand."

As Mary Anne sorted out this scheduling wrinkle, I looked around at my friends and thought about which class each of them should teach.

For Mallory, English would be a perfect fit. She loves books and writing and hopes someday to write and illustrate stories for children. She has a dry, wry sense of humor that would probably work well in books for kids.

Mallory has reddish-brown hair, glasses, braces, and a nose she hates. She complains about her looks all the time — as if looks matter. Her personality is funny and perky and she's a good person. Those are things that count.

Since she and Jessi are eleven and the rest of us are thirteen, they're our junior members. They only work during the day, unless they're sitting for their own brothers and sisters.

Speaking of Jessi, there's no doubt what class she should teach — dance. She's a graceful classical dancer who works hard at it. She even looks the part, with her long legs and her black hair swept off her face ballerina-style.

Jessi and her family moved to Stoneybrook from Oakley, New Jersey, a town with a mix of ethnic groups. So the Ramseys were shocked when here in Stoneybrook some people gave them a hard time because they're African-American. They snubbed them and were rude and basically intolerant. Fortunately, that seems to be in the past now, and the Ramseys have lots of good friends here.

"Okay, that's all set," Claudia said, hanging up the phone. "Write me in for the Pikes this Thursday at three-thirty. Mal, do you think the girls would like it if I brought over my bead-making kit?" she asked.

"They'd love it. They go wild when you bring your art stuff over."

Claudia's class would have to be art. She lives and breathes it. She even looks like art. I'm not kidding. Today she was wearing a long-sleeved white T-shirt on which she'd painted a bald man's head from a side view. All the lines were sharp, not natural at all. His nose was purple, his eyes were orange, and his skin was green. Jagged yellow lines like lightning bolts sizzled around his head. "What is that supposed to be?" I'd asked her when I saw her in school.

"A person having a great idea," she'd answered, as if it should have been obvious to me. "You, especially, should have recognized it, Ms. Idea Machine."

"I generally don't turn colors when I think. Why is his skin green?" I'd asked.

"Why not?" she'd replied. Sometimes, I have to admit, I don't get it. But Claudia is creative. She's also a junk food maniac, which is why she's been assigned to be our club caterer. (Her official title is vice-president.) As club caterer all she really has to do is pull out the bags of snacks she has hidden all over her room. (Her parents forbid her to eat the stuff. But does that stop her? N-o-o-o-o-o.)

Really, you'd never think Claudia likes junk food so much. She's slim and has perfect skin. Her long, straight black hair gleams, and there's always a shine in her dark, almond-shaped eyes. (She's Japanese-American.) Claudia is like a walking advertisement for the benefits of unhealthy eating. I wonder sometimes how long she'll be able to keep it up before something (like a zit) catches up with her.

Claudia's best friend is Stacey. The class Stacey would most like to teach is math, as she mentioned. She could also teach a special class on style and sophistication. Stacey is originally from New York City, and it shows. I think she seems older than the rest of us. (With the possible exception of Claudia.)

Stacey isn't just a former city girl. She still goes there on weekends every so often to stay with her father. You see, her parents are divorced and her dad still lives in the city. She's also dating this guy named Ethan, who's an art student there. So, in a way, Stacey has another life in New York City.

One more thing about Stacey. She's diabetic and has to eat healthily and carefully. It's serious business. Her body doesn't properly regulate the amount of sugar in her bloodstream. To keep this condition under control, she has to give herself injections of insulin every day. She also has to watch what she eats. She's very disciplined about these things and most of the time her diabetes doesn't get in the way of her life.

"Okay," Mary Anne told our group, "everyone is doing TOT except Abby, Jessi, and Claudia. Is that right?"

We nodded.

Of course it was right. Mary Anne never gets a scheduling matter wrong. Her class could be secretarial sciences. She would be a great guidance counselor too. She's an excellent listener, extremely sympathetic, and she really cares about people.

Mary Anne and I actually look a bit alike — small with brown eyes and brown hair.

Mary Anne is so sweet that people assume she's had an easy life. That's not true. Her mother died when Mary Anne was just a baby. She lived with her grandparents for awhile after that, because her dad was so freaked out that at first he couldn't deal with raising a child. Soon, though, he pulled himself together and came for her. He was a good father but very strict. Mary Anne had to fight for every little freedom she had.

In seventh grade, Mary Anne met Dawn Schafer. Dawn is tall and willowy with straight blonde hair and strong convictions about issues such as ecology. Dawn's parents had recently divorced and Mrs. Schafer had moved home to Stoneybrook, where she'd grown up.

One day, Mary Anne and Dawn discovered that their parents had been a couple when they were teenagers. They instantly began plotting to bring them together again. Amazingly, it worked. Dawn and Mary Anne became stepsisters and best friends and Mary Anne and her father moved into Dawn's old farmhouse on Burnt Hill Road. (Dawn's brother, Jeff, soon went back to California.) The Schafer-Spiers were doing pretty well as a new family until Dawn decided she missed California too. She moved back there to live with Jeff, her father, and his new wife.

We all were sad when Dawn left, but Mary Anne took it the hardest. I think she felt deserted. But she had me, her other best friend, and she also had Logan.

Logan Bruno is Mary Anne's boyfriend. He's also an associate member of the BSC. That means he doesn't come to meetings, but we call him for a job if no one else is available. I'd assign him to teach a gym class, since he's athletic and loves sports.

Our other associate member is Shannon Kilbourne. She could teach any class she wanted, since she's a real brain. In fact, we invited her become a full-time BSC member, but she is so involved with after-school activities that she couldn't give the time to the club.

After Dawn left for California (and Shannon turned down our offer to join), Abby moved to town. She lives two houses down from me, which is how we met. Almost immediately, we invited her to join the club. We also invited her identical twin sister, Anna, but she said no. Luckily, Abby said yes.

That shows you how different they are, despite the fact that they both have curly dark hair, dark brown eyes, and the same even, slightly pointy features. Abby's hair is long, while Anna's is short. Abby prefers to use contact lenses, and Anna wears glasses. Abby is athletic. Anna is musical. Abby has asthma and lots of allergies. Anna doesn't, but she does have to wear a brace for the next few years because of a curved spine condition called scoliosis. (She wears it under her clothing and you hardly notice it.)

Abby's class could be gym. But she could also teach a class in comedy. She's always making wisecracks and puns.

Things haven't always been so funny for Abby, though. When she was nine, her father died in a car accident. She says she barely even smiled back in those days. That was when the Stevensons lived on Long Island.

After Mr. Stevenson's death, life was hard for everyone in the household. But slowly, Anna and Abby began to laugh and enjoy things again. Their mother kicked her career as an editor into high gear, worked super-hard, and was promoted to an important executive editorial position. People call her a workaholic. Personally, I think that's an unfair label to put on someone who loves his or her job and gives everything to it. Abby complains, though, that she doesn't see as much of her mother as she'd like to.

"Hello . . . Kristy?" Stacey was waving her hand in front of my face.

I'd been so involved in my thoughts that I hadn't been paying attention, which isn't like me. "Sorry. What?" I said.

"I asked you if you thought it would be all right to spend the club dues on a new notebook. This one's full. And we need new Kid-Kit supplies."

The BSC notebook is a journal in which we write down what happens on each sitting job we take. It was my idea, and a lot of the members wish I hadn't thought of it. They think it's a chore, except for Mallory. But it's important that everyone knows what's going on with all our clients. Say, for instance, a kid is afraid of the dark. A sitter can read the notebook before going to the job and she might think to bring along a special night-light or to play flashlight tag. Little things like this make us very popular and effective sitters.

"Definitely get a new notebook," I agreed.

"What about the Kid-Kits?" Stacey asked. Each of us has a box of fun stuff — art supplies, stickers, little toys, etc. — that we bring on sitting jobs that might be difficult.

"Is everybody low on supplies?" I asked.

"Pretty much," Stacey reported. "We can afford to give everyone five dollars toward new stuff."

I nodded. "Okay. I don't need anything, though. I still have enough."

The phone rang again. It was Dr. Johanssen, looking for a sitter on Thursday afternoon for her daughter, Charlotte. "There's no one who can do it," Mary Anne said without having to check the record book. "Abby, Jessi, and Claudia are busy, and the rest of us will be at TOT training."

"Better call Logan or Shannon," I suggested.

"Okay," Mary Anne said. "But I'm pretty sure Logan wants to do TOT too. We should call Shannon first." Thank goodness Shannon doesn't go to SMS. She attends a private school called Stoneybrook Day School. Hopefully, they weren't doing TOT there this week.

It turned out that Shannon was at the Stevensons' house, since Anna and Shannon are good friends. Abby phoned her there and she agreed to sit for Charlotte. (There's nothing I hate more than having to turn down a client, especially a steady one like Dr. Johanssen. I always worry that the client won't call back again.)

"I can't wait until Monday to sign up for TOT," Mallory said eagerly. "I'd love to teach a class on poetry. Maybe I'll be able to do Emily Dickinson. Lately I've been reading her poems and they're so amazing."

"Slow down," Claudia said with a laugh. "What if you have to teach an algebra lesson?"

Mallory giggled. "I'll write a poem about it." She put her hand over her heart and a dreamy expression came over her face as she began to recite. "The value of X?/What could it be?/This I'll say/Don't ask me."

Everyone laughed. "Oh, I'm sure the math teacher will adore that," Stacey teased.

"You're right," Mallory agreed. "It might not be the best thing to do. Keep your fingers crossed that I get to teach an English class."

CHAPTER 3

On Monday morning I spotted a sign in the school lobby that read TOT VOLUNTEER SIGN-UP IN CAFETERIA TODAY.

"See you later," I said to Abby, who takes the bus with me to school. "I'm going in right now."

"I can't believe you're so psyched about this," she said, shaking her head.

"I can't believe you're not," I replied as I headed for the cafeteria. I entered it and found the sign-up table to my right. Mallory was already there. "Hi," I said. "Where's everyone else?"

"They wanted to get to their lockers first," she explained, "but I couldn't wait."

"Me neither."

Behind the table were Mr. Zizmore, a math teacher, and Mrs. Amer, a guidance counselor. "They're the TOT coordinators," Mallory told me.

We stood together, watching, as kids filled

out the forms on the table. Cokie Mason was there. So was her friend Grace Blume. Alan Gray was filling out a form — the head lunatic, eager to take over.

"I can't believe those kids want to do this," I commented in a low voice. "They barely do their own schoolwork. Why would they want to teach?"

"Extra credit," Mallory reminded me.

"Yeah. They probably need as much of it as they can get. Besides, I know Cokie views this as a chance to miss her own classes."

A boy with dirty blond hair approached the sign-up table. "Cary Retlin!" I gasped. "Oh, no! Can you imagine *him* as your teacher?"

"You probably wouldn't have to do much work," Mallory observed.

Cary Retlin and the BSC have a bit of a history. In his cool, mellow way, Cary has decided that it's his role in life to keep the BSC from becoming "complacent and boring." As if he even has a clue about what we do and how boring we are *not*.

Mallory clutched my arm. "What if I'm in a class Cary Retlin is teaching?" she asked, her eyes wide with horror.

"Just hope you're out teaching another class," I replied.

Cary must have sensed that we were talking

about him. He looked up from the form he was filling out and grinned.

"Why does he always act like he's got some private embarrassing secret he knows about you?" I fumed.

"That's just how he is," Mallory said.

We waited for him to clear out (which he did with an irritating wave in our direction) and then we approached the table. "Here you go, girls," Mrs. Amer said, handing us each a form.

Mallory and I sat on some nearby folding chairs and began to work on the form. There wasn't too much to fill out — name, address, stuff like that. Then a question followed: why are you interested in the TOT program?

I wrote what I honestly felt. *During my time here at SMS I've seen some teaching I thought could be improved. I'd like to show how I think classes should be run.*

I glanced over at Mallory's sheet to see what she'd written. *I hope to share my great love of books, reading, and literature with my fellow students.*

That made sense. What did I want to share? I wondered. My love of . . . *what?* Sports, I guessed. SMS didn't offer a business management class or a course in baby-sitting. So sports would have to be it.

I would especially love to teach in the athletic de-

partment, I added to my form, *since that is an area that I particularly enjoy.*

Mallory and I handed in our sheets, then raced to homeroom. At the end of the corridor, we went our separate ways. As I hurried toward my locker, I noticed that the hall seemed unusually empty. Everyone must already be in homeroom. I knew I had only a minute to get to mine, so I began to run.

"Ms. Thomas!" a voice behind me bellowed like an army drill sergeant. I froze and slowly turned to face Ms. Walden, one of the gym teachers. "Why are you running in the hall?"

She made it sound as if she'd caught me stealing a car.

I smiled anxiously. "I'm late."

She folded her arms. "Why is that?"

"Oh, because I was signing up for the TOT program," I said enthusiastically.

"That is no excuse for running in the hallway," she barked.

"Sorry," I said, even though I was more annoyed than sorry. What was the big deal? There wasn't even anyone else in the hall. All right, it was the rule — no running — and I'd broken it. She was right. I knew that. Still . . .

My annoyance must have been apparent because Ms. Walden shot me a hard, angry look. "Get to class," she said. "And *walk*!"

I walked away, feeling her cold stare digging

into the back of my head. What I resented most was being treated like a baby. A baby and a criminal — at the same time.

Once I turned the hallway corner, I was tempted to run again. But I didn't dare. Instead, I race-walked to my locker, grabbed my books, and race-walked to homeroom.

As I hurried along, I thought about how great it would be to teach. Then I'd be the one calling the shots, not the one being bossed around by people like Ms. Walden.

Last year she'd been my gym teacher and I'd thought I liked her. I defended her to the kids who hated her. And there were a lot of them, believe me.

Now I thought that those kids might have had a point. Maybe she really *was* overbearing and tyrannical. Maybe it was just my love of sports that had made me try to like her.

In truth, she picked on the kids who weren't athletic. She yelled all the time. And sometimes she expected us to perform impossible feats, such as sinking five free-throw baskets in a row during the basketball unit.

I resolved then and there that if I were assigned a gym class, Ms. Walden would be my model for how *not* to teach.

CHAPTER 4

"Ms. Walden!" I gasped that Thursday when we received our teaching assignments. I was with the other volunteers in the auditorium, waiting for our first session of student teacher training to begin.

I'd just been handed a slip of paper saying I would be student teaching for Ms. Walden during her seventh-grade gym class. Yikes!

Stacey was in the second row seat to my right. "Ms. Walden? That crab? Oh, well. You can show her it's possible to run a gym class and still be a nice person."

That's true, I thought. A picture flashed in my mind — kids smiling and having fun in my gym class; Ms. Walden in the background, watching carefully, vowing to herself to be nicer to the kids in the future.

"Who do you have?" I asked Stacey.

"Seventh-grade math," she reported with a pleased expression. "Mr. Peters's class."

"He's okay," I commented. "I had him last year."

Mary Anne leaned forward from a seat in the row behind Stacey. "I got seventh-grade social studies, Mr. Redmont," she said.

"That's good," Stacey remarked. "Is it what you wanted?"

"Yup."

I noticed Mallory sitting beside Mary Anne. She was slumped in her seat and scowling at the paper in her lap. "Didn't you get English?" I asked.

She nodded but didn't look up from her paper. "I got it," she mumbled.

"Then what's the — " I was interrupted by Mr. Zizmore, who had walked to the front of the auditorium and stood in the center aisle.

"Attention, everyone, and welcome to the Teachers of Tomorrow Training Seminar," he announced. "The first thing we will talk about is how to create a lesson plan."

I didn't think this would apply to me. How much of a lesson plan would you need to teach a gym class? While Mr. Zizmore spoke, I gazed around at the other volunteers to see who had signed up. Nearly fifty kids had.

At first I was impressed by the number. I was surprised so many students were interested. But, as I continued to watch them, I grew a lot more skeptical.

While Mr. Zizmore explained the lesson plan, Alan Gray was sailing paper airplanes across the room. Cokie Mason was applying makeup. Cary was using a piece of paper to create static electricity in the hair of the girl in front of him, Kara Mauricio. She kept giggling and batting him away, but not as if she really meant it.

Hopeless, I thought, looking around. If these kids were the Teachers of Tomorrow, then I felt sorry for the students of tomorrow.

"You will have to stay on the topic the teacher for your particular class is teaching," Mr. Zizmore said.

"You mean I can't teach creative paper folding?" Alan Gray called out, holding up his paper airplane.

"Not unless you are teaching an art class on origami," Mr. Zizmore replied. Stacey smiled at that one. She loves Mr. Z. "But that brings up an excellent point, Alan," he continued.

I laughed to myself. Alan was trying to be a wise guy, and Mr. Zizmore had turned things around so that it seemed as if Alan were making excellent points.

"You will have a great deal of flexibility within your given unit," Mr. Zizmore continued. "For example, if you are assigned a literature class, you can decide what story or poem you will teach."

I glanced over my shoulder at Mallory, thinking she'd be happy to hear this news. I tried to make eye contact, but she was still staring down at her assignment paper as if she couldn't believe what she was seeing.

Mr. Zizmore asked someone to turn down the lights. On a screen on the stage, he projected a slide showing an enlarged lesson plan. Different slides highlighted the various aspects of the lesson plan.

The amount of time spent on each part of the subject was broken into fifteen-minute segments. The plan he showed indicated fifteen minutes for teaching a lesson on the history of World War I, then ten minutes for class discussion, five minutes for the class to write a quick response to the question "What was the immediate cause of World War I?", then a final fifteen minutes discussing the difference between immediate causes and background causes of a war. A fast-moving forty-five–minute class.

"With this kind of plan you don't fall behind," Mr. Zizmore explained in the darkened auditorium. He flipped to the next slide, which showed how this plan was laid out in a lesson-plan book — a special notebook designed especially for teachers. The slide after that showed a blank lesson-plan page.

"With a lesson plan, you also keep up a lively pace. You don't become stuck on one aspect of a subject. And a lesson plan helps you make sure you are meeting state curriculum requirements."

He snapped on the lights. "We teachers periodically turn in our lesson plans. Mr. Kingbridge checks to see that each teacher is on target covering the curriculum for that year. You too will have to turn in your lesson plans to your master teacher."

Alan Gray called out, "Yes, *massssterrr*," as if he were Igor speaking to Dracula.

Mr. Zizmore ignored him and continued to talk about how we should construct our lesson plans. "Be realistic about how much time you will need," he suggested.

I found this fascinating. With my admiration for organization, I was truly impressed with this system. I still couldn't see how it would apply to a gym class, but I wondered if I could use it for the BSC. Could I get each member a lesson planner and ask her to chart how she intended to use her time during jobs? It might be very useful. But could you actually chart babysitting time as you would class time?

I became caught up in this question and stopped listening to Mr. Zizmore. I had the basic idea of it anyway, and didn't need to go over it a million times. (Although it was probably a good idea for Mr. Z. to repeat it for kids like Cokie and Alan.)

Could a lesson plan be used effectively in the BSC? I came up with reasons why it could — games could be planned, TV viewing charted, kids' homework time accounted for, suppers served on time, etc. There were also reasons why it couldn't — kids don't always like schedules, they ask for extra stories, want to see extra TV, get sick, quarrel, fool around, and so on. Besides that, we'd have to budget for everyone to have lesson planners, which would continually need to be replaced.

In the end I decided lesson planners would not work in the BSC. My timing was good. Just as I decided this, Mr. Zizmore dismissed the group. "See you all tomorrow for session two," he said.

Immediately I swung around in my seat. "*What* is the matter, Mallory?" I demanded. I reached out and took the paper from her hands.

I saw the problem right away. Mallory had been assigned to Mrs. Simon — to *my* English class — which meant they'd given a sixth-grader an eighth-grade English class.

"That's a compliment," I said, handing the paper back to her. "They must think you're a brilliant English student."

"Eighth grade?" Mary Anne asked.

"Maybe it's a mistake," Stacey suggested. "You should check with Mr. Z."

Mallory's expression brightened as she bolted from her chair and hurried to the front of the room. Mary Anne, Stacey, and I watched while she spoke to him. Mr. Zizmore was shaking his head, and Mal looked more and more despondent by the second.

"No mistake, huh," I said as she slouched back to us.

"No. What am I going to do? An eighth-grade class won't listen to me. This is horrible."

"I'll be there," I said. "Mary Anne too. We'll make sure it goes all right."

That seemed to help. Mallory smiled. "Okay," she said. "Thanks."

Now it was the look on Mary Anne's face that worried me. She bit her lip and frowned at me as if to say, *Why did you promise something we can't do?*

CHAPTER 5

Thursday

I that I was not doing TOT but it terned out that I did it any way. Vanesa did her own vershun of the program. It was a strang vershun, but Clair and margo had fun.

That afternoon, while Abby was at the allergist, Jessi was at her ballet class, and the rest of us were at TOT training, Claudia sat for Vanessa (age nine), Margo (seven), and Claire Pike (five).

The moment Mrs. Pike left, Vanessa swung into action. She popped up from the floor, where she'd been lying between Claire and Margo, watching TV. "Mallory may be a TOT. But all alone she is not," Vanessa sang out dramatically. "I can be a teacher too, and —" she pointed to her younger sisters — I am planning on teaching *you*!"

"Nice poem," Claudia said, laughing. Like Mallory, Vanessa also wants to be a writer. Her specialty is poetry.

Claire leaped to her feet. "You're teaching us?" she cried eagerly. "What are you teaching us?"

"Poetry, of course," Vanessa replied.

Margo ducked her head and covered it with her hands. "Oh, no-o-o," she mumbled.

Vanessa straddled her sister and pulled her up by the shoulders. "No hiding. You need to learn about poetry."

Claire turned off the TV. "Come on, Margo, come on. It's fun to play school.

"Oh, all right," Margo grumbled as she rolled away from Vanessa. "You'll both bug me until I do it anyway." She looked at Claudia. "Are you going to play?"

"Sure," Claudia agreed. Normally, school wouldn't be a game she'd suggest, but she thought that maybe Vanessa's version would be fun.

Vanessa instructed her students to sit on the couch while she ran upstairs.

"I'm learning to write in school," Claire proudly told Claudia. "I can spell some words. Cat, C-A-T. Dog, D-O-G. House, H-O-S-E."

"Very good." Claudia applauded.

"Why did you say good?" Margo demanded. "She spelled house wrong."

"Did not!" Claire shot back.

"Did too!"

The girls looked to Claudia to solve the argument. "Well . . ." she began.

"If you spell mouse, M-O-U-S-E, then house has to be spelled H-O-U-S-E because it rhymes with mouse," Margo insisted.

"Did someone say rhymes?" Vanessa asked as she scurried down the stairs. She was holding a piece of light blue poster board in one hand and a box of colored markers in the other.

"I said *house* rhymes with *mouse*, so it must be spelled the same," Margo explained. "Isn't that right?"

"No," Vanessa said with a knowledgeable shake of her head. "I mean it might, but it doesn't have to. Anyway, it doesn't matter. Spelling is totally unimportant."

"It is?" Claire squinted her eyes at Vanessa. That wasn't what she'd been told in kindergarten.

"Well . . . that's what I've always felt," Claudia admitted. "But I'm not sure that — "

"Absolutely unimportant!" Vanessa maintained, swooshing a red marker dramatically through the air. "In poetry, *sound* is what matters."

"Wait a minute, Vanessa," Margo objected. "Won't everyone who reads your poems think you're dumb if they're all spelled wrong?"

"They won't be spelled wrong because someone else will fix the misspellings," Vanessa informed her.

Margo wasn't buying this. "Like who?"

"Like a secretary or an editor or someone like that," Vanessa replied. "Besides, spelling was made up by a bunch of crazy people who wrote words in the strangest ways they could think of, just to confuse everyone else."

"That's the truth!" said Claudia. *At last, someone who understands the problem*, she thought. Vanessa might only be nine, but she was on to something. At least in Claudia's opinion.

"I can spell, but I think worrying about spelling gets in the way of making great poems," Vanessa said. "The first thing you must know about a poem is that it has to rhyme."

"My teacher says it doesn't," Margo protested. "Haiku poems, written in Japan, don't rhyme."

"That's *Japanese* poetry," Vanessa replied irritably. "The rules are different in America."

"I don't think all American poems rhyme either," Claudia said gently. She remembered learning this in English class.

Vanessa stamped one foot. "My poems rhyme and that's what I'm teaching — *rhyming poems.*"

"I like rhyming poems," Claire said. "I know one — 'Little Miss Muffet/Sat on a tuffet/Eating her curds and whey . . .' " She stopped and made a confused face. "What's a tuffet?"

"And what's curds and whey?" Margo asked.

Claudia shrugged. "I've always wondered about that myself."

"A tuffet is something you sit on and curds and whey are something you eat," Vanessa said in a patient voice.

Margo scowled at her. "We knew that! What we wanted to know was — "

" 'Miss Muffet' is a nice poem, Claire," Vanessa cut her off. "But it's not a *great* poem. In my class, you will learn to make up great poems that express your true feelings." She propped her poster board against the TV and used her marker to print the word *fly*. "Today we will make a poem by rhyming the word *fly*. Class, what rhymes with fly?"

"Sky!" Claire shouted.

"My," Margo said.

"Eskimo pie," Claudia offered.

"Very good," Vanessa commended them. She wrote their suggestions on her poster board. "Now more suggestions."

After they filled the board with rhyming words, they worked together to compose a poem using them. Claudia told me she had a great time. If real school were as much fun as Vanessa's school, Claudia might not mind attending.

At five-thirty, Mrs. Pike returned with Mallory, whom she'd picked up at school. As they walked through the door, Mrs. Pike was saying to Mal, "You're so good at English, I'm sure it won't make a bit of difference to the eighth-graders that — "

She was cut off by Claire, who hurled herself excitedly into her mother. "Mom, oh, Mom, how the time does fly/Just moments ago we said good-bye/Did you bring home an Eskimo pie?/Did you even try? I say with a sigh/I want to cry/No Eskimo pie/For poor little I."

Mrs. Pike stared at Claire, stunned.

Mallory's hand flew to her cheek. "Oh, no, Mom! She's turned into another Vanessa!"

Margo joined them and began to recite. "Why, oh, why do the songbirds fly?/Soaring so lovely up in the sky/Wish I could too — I try/I try/But no wings have I with which to fly."

Mallory turned to Claudia, who stood beside the very pleased-looking Vanessa. "Claudia, what did you do to them?" she cried.

Claudia grinned as she replied, "To false conclusions do not fly/It 'twas Vanessa, but not I."

CHAPTER 6

Friday afternoon, after school, my friends and I arrived at the auditorium, ready for our second day of training. We expected Mr. Zizmore to be there. Maybe Mrs. Amer too. What we didn't expect was the fifty or more teachers who sat waiting for us.

Mr. Zizmore quieted everyone down and then spoke. "Today you will meet with your master teacher to discuss the class you will be teaching," he explained.

I glanced at Ms. Walden. She sat with her arms folded, wearing a bland expression. She must have known, by now, that I was her student teacher. It would have been nice if she had nodded or smiled at me.

After our unpleasant meeting in the hall the other day, I didn't know what to expect. How would she feel about my teaching her seventh-grade gym class? Did she suspect that I'd take them all for a run down the hall?

Of course she didn't. But still . . . did she think I'd be a bad influence on the class?

Yesterday, when I'd gotten the assignment, I'd told myself it didn't matter. I could handle Ms. Walden. Now, though, looking at her face, it seemed a little scarier.

"All right, students please find your teachers," Mr. Zizmore instructed.

Seats creaked as everyone stood up. I noticed Mallory stepping from side to side nervously as she spoke to my English teacher, Mrs. Simon.

"Thomas," a voice barked from behind me. I knew it was Ms. Walden.

"Hello, Ms. Walden," I said, forcing a smile.

"So, you'll be teaching my class," she said flatly, taking me in with her steely eyes. "Sit down. I'm going to give you a few tips you'll find helpful."

I nodded and sat.

"First of all, don't expect much from these girls," she advised. "This group isn't especially athletic."

Maybe if they had a teacher who believed in them they'd do better, I thought. What an attitude — the girls can't do anything so don't even try. How awful!

"Second," she continued, "some of them will try to fool you. They'll say they feel sick or they hurt their ankle. Things like that. Don't believe them. It's just a con job."

If the class was fun they might not be so desperate to escape.

"I don't think it will be a big problem," I commented.

Ms. Walden's eyes narrowed. "Don't be so sure," was all she said.

"Third," she went on, "keep firm discipline at all times. The moment you let the class get out of control, it's all over. Gym isn't like other classes, where students are confined to their desks. There's room to move in a gym, and that inspires kids to act up. Don't let them. Keep them busy and keep them in line."

With her attitude, it was no wonder she had problems with the class. Hopefully, she'd learn a better way to deal with the students after she watched me. No matter what I did, it *had* to be better than the way she was conducting this class.

"We're working on the soccer unit," she told me. "As I recall, you're a good player."

"Pretty good."

"Don't expect the same of them," she said. "There are one or two decent players. I suspect some of them may be more athletic than they let on. I heard that a few of them take karate."

Things would be different once I was teaching. I was used to helping kids along. You should see some of the Krushers. *Bad* didn't even begin to describe them, at least in the beginning. But I've learned that even bad players have a lot of potential. You just need some patience and an upbeat attitude.

For the next half hour, Ms. Walden told me exactly how she wanted the class run — every last detail. She insisted I make sure the students were wearing the proper gym suit and sneakers. She told me exactly when she required them lined up to go out to the field. She told me what indoor soccer exercises to do if it rained. And on and on.

About halfway through I stopped listening. I had no intention of doing things Ms. Walden's way. Her way was the way that caused students to pretend to be sick. *My* way would show them they were better than they knew, and that gym could be fun and rewarding.

"Are you getting this?" Ms. Walden asked sharply, snapping me back to attention.

"Yes," I answered. "Definitely."

"Good. There's something else you should be aware of. For this unit we're working with Mr. De Young's class." (He's one of the boys' gym teachers — a pretty nice guy.) "That means you'll have to coordinate your lesson plan with the student teacher for that class."

"No problem," I assured her. "Who's that?"

"Cary Retlin."

Cary Retlin! I hoped I'd heard her wrong.

I glanced over Ms. Walden's shoulder. Cary was talking with Mr. De Young.

No, I hadn't heard wrong.

At that moment, Mr. De Young must have told Cary I'd be his partner. Cary looked around the auditorium and spotted me gaping at him in horror.

In response, he grinned the most obnoxious, self-satisfied, irritating grin I've ever seen in my life.

"What's the matter, Kristy?" Mary Anne asked me at our BSC meeting that afternoon. "Are you still upset about teaching with Cary Retlin?"

"I think I'm in shock," I told her. "My hands are cold. I'm not thinking clearly. Those are symptoms of shock, aren't they?"

"Yes," Stacey said, "but don't worry, Kristy. Let Cary know who's boss. You can handle him."

"I'm the one who should be in shock," Mallory insisted. "Mrs. Simon told me not to worry, but I don't know. What if they think I'm a total dweeb?"

"You're not a total dweeb, so don't worry about it," I told her.

"It'll be fine," Mary Anne said. "I'm excited about this. Mr. Redmont was so nice. I'm not half as nervous as I was before I spoke to him."

"Mr. Peters was great too," Stacey said. "This is going to be a blast."

"Even though I didn't want to teach, I'm looking forward to being the student of a student," Abby put in. "It'll be a change, anyway."

"It has to be better than regular class," Claudia said as she bit into a Ring-Ding. "Alan Gray is teaching my social studies class. Can you imagine what a circus that's going to be? I can't wait."

"You *want* Alan to teach the class?" I asked.

"It beats working," Claudia replied.

Mallory let out a long, sick moan.

"What?" Jessi asked.

"Beats working! That's what the eighth-graders are going to say when they see me walk in. They'll destroy me. They'll goof off. They won't listen. I'll be so embarrassed, I'll want to disappear."

"Mallory, you're a great baby-sitter," I reminded her. "The kids you sit for always listen to you. This isn't going to be so different."

"Of course it's going to be different," Mallory disagreed. Her voice was becoming more shrill by the moment. "These aren't eight-year-olds — they're eighth-graders!"

I said a few more things, trying to sound encouraging. It seemed the right thing to do. But I wasn't being completely honest. If I were in her shoes, I'd have been just as panicked.

CHAPTER 7

"Are you ready for your big day?" Abby asked as she slid into the seat beside me on the bus Monday morning.

"Sure," I replied.

"You've got your lesson plan and everything all mapped out?"

"Not on paper, exactly."

"Aren't you supposed to submit a lesson plan? That's what Anna was doing all weekend — writing up this lesson plan like she was concocting blueprints for a nuclear reactor. Hers is incredibly detailed."

"Anna is teaching music. Gym is totally different," I replied.

"If you say so."

"Well, it *is*. There's too much movement in sports to chart it all down on paper. You can't know what's going to happen until it gets going. Ms. Walden knows that. I bet she never makes a lesson plan. If she really wants something on paper, I'll do it at lunch and hand it in afterward. At least by then I'll know what happened and how long it all took."

"I don't think that's the idea," Abby replied. "You're supposed to use it to control how long everything takes. That's what Anna says."

"I told you, Anna is teaching music." I didn't want to talk about it anymore. Abby wasn't even in the program. Why was she giving me such a hard time? I *liked* the idea of lesson plans, just not for gym class.

Besides, I had other things on my mind. On Sunday afternoon, I'd finally called Cary. It was a chore and I'd kept putting off.

As if she were reading my mind, Abby asked, "Have you talked to Cary about this yet?"

"I tried to. But he's so weird. He actually asked me what the goalie does in soccer."

Abby's eyes widened in disbelief. Then she smiled. "He was busting your chops."

"I don't think so."

"Sure he was. Who doesn't know what a goalie is? We've all played soccer in gym. Even if you don't know any other position, you know the goalie. He just wanted to make you crazy."

"He succeeded," I muttered. "He thinks TOT is a big goof!"

"He treats a lot of things that way," Abby reminded me. "Sometimes he's kind of funny."

"Yeah, well, you're not stuck with him. I am."

"Just keep a sense of humor about him and you'll be all right," she advised. I decided she was probably right. If I led the way and didn't take him too seriously, I could survive this.

When I reached my locker, I found Mallory waiting there, shifting anxiously from one foot to the other. "Hi," I said.

She spoke in a shaky, nervous voice. "Kristy, what can you tell me about the class? I need to know what the kids are like. Maybe if I know I'll be prepared."

"They're the usual mix," I told her. "Some jerks, some angels, most in the middle."

"It's the middle kids that make me nervous," Mallory said tensely. "They could go either way. If I start to stumble or forget something, they'll band together with the jerks. Then I'll be faced with a majority of jerks, all united against me." As she spoke, she actually grew pale. For a second, I worried that she might faint.

I grabbed her shoulders. "Hold on, Mallory. Calm down. You're prepared, aren't you?"

She flipped open her three-ring binder. "I . . . I think so." She turned the binder around so that I could see what she had. "Twenty-four photocopies of 'The Jumblies' by Edward Lear. It wouldn't have been my first choice, but Mrs.

Simon wanted to cover story poems, and this one is a story poem."

"It sounds interesting," I said.

Mallory shot me a twitchy half smile, then continued showing me her papers. "I also made twenty-four copies of my notes about the poem. And here are pages of biographical information on Lear, and some limericks Lear wrote. Do you think I have enough?"

I laughed. "Mallory, the class is only forty-five minutes long. Of course you have enough. Don't worry. Mary Anne and I will ask questions. We'll be helpful."

"Okay. All right," she said, trying desperately to reassure herself. "It will be fine. It will."

"Sure it will," I said. I saw kids hurrying to class. "We'd better get to homeroom before we're late."

"Homeroom?" Mallory repeated vaguely.

"Yes, you remember homeroom," I said with a smile. "The first class of every school day."

Mallory laughed nervously. "Oh, yeah, homeroom." She wandered off in the direction of her homeroom.

Wow! I thought. *I've never seen such a bad case of nerves.*

When it came time to teach my gym class, I felt pretty calm. Why be nervous? This was something I could handle.

I arrived at the locker room early, since I didn't think it was very teacherly to change with the students. I didn't put on my regular gym outfit either. The gym teachers didn't wear the same T-shirt and shorts we wore, so why should I?

I wore plaid pleated shorts and a white short-sleeve polo shirt. Over the weekend I'd woven a blue-and-white lanyard and attached a whistle to it. I wore it around my neck like the other gym teachers did. I'd even gone over my sneakers with some white shoe polish so that they'd be super-white, like Ms. Walden's sneakers.

I glanced at myself in the mirror and was pleased with my appearance. I looked exactly like . . . a gym teacher. Perfect.

The seventh-grade girls began entering the locker room. A few of them looked familiar. Some peered at me curiously. One girl asked, "Are you the TOT teacher?"

"Yes, that's me," I said. "We're going to have a great class."

She rolled her eyes and several girls giggled.

"You'll see," I assured her. "This will be the best gym class you ever had."

"Yeah, sure." She turned toward her locker.

I wasn't going to let some some snippy seventh-grader rattle me. I went to the phys. ed. office in the locker room and took out the boom box the teachers use whenever music is needed. Since I was now, technically, part of the phys. ed. staff, I didn't think I needed permission.

Holding the box with one hand and twirling my whistle with the other, I walked out the locker room door and into the gym, where I met Cary. He was slumped against the wall, his arms folded.

"Oh, hello, Kristin," he said, pushing away from the wall. (He knows very well that everyone calls me Kristy.) "You're just the person I wanted to see."

"Hello, Cary," I replied. "Why did you want to see me?"

I put the boom box near an outlet and kept walking, thinking it was best to make him follow me. You know — to set the tone for the rest of class.

He fell into step just behind me as I headed for the middle of the gym. "After our friendly phone call yesterday, I got the idea that maybe you might not want to work with me. That maybe you don't even like me."

His observation shocked me. I didn't realize I'd been so obvious. It was probably better to smooth things over right away. I *did* have to work with the guy, after all. "Oh, I wouldn't say — "

"I don't want to work with you either."

The out-and-out insult took me by surprise. I stopped walking and whirled toward him. "Fine," I snapped. "Let's go tell Ms. Walden and Mr. De Young that we won't be working together."

"Fine," he agreed with a smug smile, as if this were all very humorous. "Let's do that."

I charged over to the gym teachers, who were standing at the other end of the gym. I had the annoying sense that Cary was mimicking my walk. From the corner of my eye I saw him taking long steps and swinging his arms in an exaggerated way. Any time I stopped short and turned sharply to him he stopped and smirked infuriatingly at me.

I tried to ignore him and continued on to the teachers. "Ms. Walden," I began, "Cary would rather not work with me and that is completely okay."

Mr. De Young stared hard at Cary. "Is that so, Retlin?"

"Yeah, I don't think it would work," Cary replied.

"It wouldn't," I agreed. "So we'll keep our classes separate."

"No," Ms. Walden said. "Mr. De Young and I work together on this unit, and that's how we want it taught."

"This is *our* class, isn't it?" I objected. "*We're* the teachers."

"But it's going to be taught jointly." Ms. Walden's tone made it plain that there was no room for further discussion. "Teachers, your class is assembled," she said, nodding toward the students behind us.

I turned and saw that the students had gathered in the gym. They ambled around, talking and joking with one another.

"You're stuck with me, Kristin," Cary commented.

Ignoring him, I headed toward the students. A blast of my whistle brought them to attention. "Hello, everyone. I'll be teaching your class today."

"*We'll* be teaching the class," Cary corrected me.

"A girl? Teaching boys' gym?" a boy called out.

"Don't freak," Cary told him. "I'm *your* teacher. Girls, you *can* freak out because you're now under the control of hammer-fisted Kristin, the Soccer Queen."

I glared at him. Then I smiled warmly at the girls. "Hi, everybody," I said. "Today we'll be playing soccer. But first, our warm-up."

Ms. Walden started all her classes with a military-style workout, complete with jumping jacks and squat thrusts. Everyone hated it.

"I've put together a new warm-up routine," I told them. "You'll find it way more fun than what you usually do."

As I spoke, I moved toward the boom box. I took the tape I was going to play from my shorts pocket, *Hits from the 70s*. Mom had let me borrow it. "Everybody, just do what I do. Follow me," I instructed.

When I clicked the tape on, a funky, upbeat song called "Joy to the World!" blared from the speakers. I began clapping over my head while I kicked out one foot, then the other. It was a move I'd seen over the weekend on an exercise show.

Everyone stood there, staring at me as if I were out of my mind. "Come on!" I encouraged them. "Clap!"

"Yes, kiddies, clap your little hands," Cary said. With a ridiculous expression on his face he clapped and bounced in a circle. Some kids found this hysterical and followed his example. The others stood with arms folded, looking peeved.

I blasted my whistle. "Be serious!" I cried. "Do what I'm doing." I began my next move, a light jog done while touching my hands to my shoulders and then stretching my arms out. A few girls began to jog along with me. "That's it!" I encouraged them. "Keep those arms up high."

The girls in front of me were cooperating so well that I didn't notice what was happening on the other side of the class. But in a minute, I couldn't miss it.

Cary had started a conga line that snaked around the gym. The kids kicked their feet out and flung their arms in total discord, whacking one another, tripping, and falling into each other.

I looked at Mr. De Young and Ms. Walden, certain that they'd call a stop to this. They just stood there, watching. They were leaving the class up to me.

I blew my whistle. "Stop!" I shouted with as much lung power as I could.

But the conga line kept right on dancing.

CHAPTER 8

At lunch that day I sat with my head cradled in my hands. "It was a nightmare," I told my friends. "And when we went outside for the actual soccer game, it got even worse. Cary picked up the ball and ran around the field with it. The kids began chasing him."

"That's awful. What did you do?" Stacey asked.

"I blew my whistle and blew and blew until they *finally* paid attention. Then I made them all do jumping jacks, just to bring them under control."

Abby gazed at me doubtfully. "And they actually listened to you?"

"Well, I had help. Mr. De Young came out just then and finally he stepped in. He told the class to do what I said or they'd do nothing *but* jumping jacks for the rest of the year."

"Boy, I bet they hated you for that," Abby said.

I scowled at her. "They did not. I think a lot of the kids were glad that someone was bringing some sanity back into the class. What bugs me is that I know I could have done a good job if Cary hadn't been there. The warm-up would have gone well if he hadn't started that dumb conga line. And I could have taught soccer too if he hadn't started running with the ball."

"You're going to have to have a serious talk with him before the next class," Mary Anne said.

"Tell me about it," I muttered. "I've already made one suggestion that he agreed with. Next class, he's going to coach one team and I'll coach the other."

"That's brilliant," Claudia said. "That way it will seem like you're teaching together, but you'll really be rivals."

"Exactly. I hope we annihilate his team," I added.

"Kristy, you need to lighten up," Abby said. "I think you're taking this too seriously."

"You weren't there," I snapped. "You weren't completely undercut by a total jerk."

"That's true. Still . . . it isn't like this is your real job. It's just, you know, *school*."

"I want to show Ms. Walden how she can improve the class, and thanks to Cary Retlin I can't get anything done. I don't think it's funny."

"Don't worry. Ms. Walden will know what

you had in mind when she reads your lesson plan," Mary Anne said.

"I didn't do one," I mumbled.

"You didn't?" Mary Anne looked shocked. "My social studies class today went really well. But without the lesson plan to check, I wouldn't have been half as organized."

"Gym is diffcrent," I said. And in fact, Ms. Walden hadn't asked for the plan, so I assumed she agreed with me and didn't think much of lesson plans for gym.

I had English class right after lunch. I knew it would be taught by Mallory, and I figured she was a jumble of jangled nerves by now.

Mary Anne and I walked to class together. "Keep your fingers crossed for Mal," I said to her.

"I'm not worried. She's as prepared as can be."

I thought about that and felt a twinge of guilt. Should I have been more prepared? No. Who could possibly have been prepared for Cary Retlin? No matter what kind of carefully detailed lesson plan I'd written down, he'd have thrown it off track.

We arrived at the door of our English classroom and found Mallory waiting there. "Hi," I said. She wriggled her fingers at me. Her face was pale.

"Aren't you going inside?" Mary Anne asked her.

She nodded but made no move. "When?" I asked.

"N-N-Now." She didn't budge.

"Listen, Mallory," I said, "you know me, and you know Mary Anne. Teach the class as if you were speaking to us. Just focus on us, at least until you relax a little."

Mrs. Simon came to the door and smiled. "We're ready to start," she said. Mary Anne and I nudged Mallory into the classroom. She hovered by the door while we took our seats. "Class," Mrs. Simon began, "today's student teacher is Mallory Pike. She's going to talk to you about a poem called 'The Jumblies' by Edward Lear. I'm sure you'll all give her your attention and cooperation. Go ahead, Mallory."

"Thank you, Mrs. Simon," Mallory said as she moved to the middle of the room. I was pleased to hear her voice come out more forcefully than it had in the hall.

"I'm going to pass out copies of the poem for each of you," she told the class. "Please take one and pass the rest to the person behind you." She stepped up to Lily Karp, who sits in the first seat of the first row by the door. As she reached out to hand the stack to Lily, the papers tumbled from her hands and fell to the floor. This brought on a few giggles from the class. When Mallory bent to pick up the papers, another stack slid from her other hand.

That — combined with Mallory's horrified expression — caused a lot of laughter.

Mallory grabbed up the papers, but now they were a mess. "Those papers have got a bad case of 'The Jumblies'!" Pete Black called out. He's a pretty good guy and didn't mean any harm by it, but Mallory blushed a deep red.

I jumped up, took the papers from her, and began handing them out. "How cute," Cokie whispered as she took her sheet. "Helping your little buddy." I ignored her.

"As you can see," Mallory began once I sat down again, " 'The Jumblies' is a long poem. But Edward Lear is really most famous for — "

"For inventing the Lear jet!" a boy named Lane Reynolds shouted out.

At first Mallory looked surprised. Then she smiled. "No. That would have been impossible because Edward Lear was born in eighteen-twelve." She turned toward the board to write this down. I could see her hand shaking. I suppose the whole class could see it.

She turned back toward us. "He was best known for the limerick, which is a short, humorous verse form consisting of five lines. The first, second, and fifth lines rhyme, as do the third and fourth." She'd obviously memorized this and her voice had a stiff, robotic rhythm to it.

From the corner of my eye, I noticed Alan Gray wadding up a spitball. An unwrapped straw lay on his desk. I cleared my throat loudly in his direction. He glanced at me and I gave him a Look — my most deadly glare, which I reserve for times when I really want to get a point across. He got my message and held up his hand in a silent surrender sign.

I turned my attention back to Mallory and saw she was once again writing on the board. Her hands still trembled terribly as she wrote down an example of a limerick.

There was an old man who supposed
That the street door was partially closed;
But some very large rats
Ate his coats and his hats

She didn't finish the limerick because the chalk cracked with a loud snap and went flying across the classroom. "Duck!" Alan shouted, which everyone did.

"Sorry about that," Mallory said.

"What a spaz!" Cokie whispered loudly to Grace Blume.

"Spaz Girl, Spaz Girl," Grace chanted softly, giggling. Several kids looked at Mallory and laughed.

Mallory was well aware of them. She was mortified.

Mrs. Simon stood and clapped her hands sharply for silence. "There's more chalk on the right-hand side," she told Mallory.

"Don't give her another missile to attack us with!" cried Shane Miller. "We're too young to die!"

"She's armed! Look out!" Parker Harris added.

"Class!" Mrs. Simon snapped. "Be quiet and listen. I'm going to give you a quiz on this and I'll expect you to know this information."

I realized Mallory was staring hard at Mary Anne and me. She was trying to pretend we were the only two students in the room. I shot her a smile and a thumbs-up, but she didn't smile back.

"The Jumblies" is a fun poem about this group of nutty people who set out to sea in a sieve. But despite the poem, Mallory looked and sounded as if she were about to burst into tears.

Her obvious misery inspired some kids to take pity on her and ask thoughtful questions. It brought out the worst in other kids, though. They asked dumb questions and Mal knew they were goofing on her.

While she was trying to finish up the poem, I noticed a paper being passed around. It was causing a lot of laughter and I didn't want to think about what was on it. Before too long it was passed to me. Unfortunately, this is what it said:

A Limerick

There was a Spaz Girl named Mallory
She taught, but not for salary
Her joy was to aim
Deadly chalk and maim
Her students, like ducks in a shooting gallery

Each line was written in a different handwriting. It had been a joint effort among five people — five morons. I crumpled the note and crammed it into my jeans pocket.

After what seemed like the longest forty-five minutes of my life (and of Mallory's life too, I'm sure) class finally ended.

"Thank you, Mallory," Mrs. Simon said. "That was very interesting."

Mallory nodded but couldn't even manage a smile. She just walked out of the classroom.

Mary Anne and I hurried after her. When we caught up with her, tears were pooled in her eyes, ready to splash over. "It wasn't that bad," Mary Anne said, which was a fib, of course, but for a good cause.

"It was," Mallory insisted in a choked voice.

"Hey, my class was a disaster too," I told her. "Maybe all first classes bomb."

Mallory took off her glasses and wiped her eyes. "Do you think so?"

"Sure," I said. At least, I hoped so. Even though my class had been bad, hers had been much worse. Anger welled up inside me. You'd think a bunch of eighth-graders would give a break to a poor kid who was two years younger than they were.

About six or seven kids from Mrs. Simon's class came down the hall. Cokie and Grace were among them. A boy's voice loudly whispered "Spaz Girl!" as they passed.

Mal turned an even deeper red than she had in the classroom.

I wanted to murder whoever had said it, but I had no idea who it was.

CHAPTER 9

Monday

Vanessa has teaching fever. It's as if the Pike house is now The Vanessa School of Poetry — and the Pike kids are her captive students whether they like it or not!

After school that day, Mallory was supposed to baby-sit at her house along with Stacey. But since Mal was desperate to speak to Mrs. Simon about the class she'd taught, Jessi agreed to replace her. (Jordan was sick in bed, so an extra sitter was needed.)

Jessi and Stacey arrived at the Pikes' and found Vanessa assembling her students. "Everyone on the couch," she commanded.

Margo ran behind Stacey. "Save me from her," she pleaded in an urgent whisper. "She hasn't stopped since last Thursday when Claudia was here. She really thinks she's a teacher."

Mrs. Pike entered the room and sized up the situation. "Margo, you don't have to play school with Vanessa if you don't want to," she said as she took her jacket from the front hall.

"She makes me, Mom," Margo replied. "She follows me all over the house until I agree to be her student."

"Vanessa," Mrs. Pike called into the living room.

Vanessa looked at her mother and then turned back to Nicky and Claire, who were sitting on the couch like obedient students. "Excuse me, class," she said to them. "I have to have a word with the principal. I'll return in a moment."

Vanessa joined her mother in the hall. "Yes, Principal Pike?"

"Vanessa, I know this is a fun game," Mrs. Pike said, "but remember, it's only a game. And if Margo doesn't want to be your student, she doesn't have to be."

Vanessa studied Margo for a moment. "All right," she agreed.

"Good," Mrs. Pike said. "I'm going to be at the elementary school, watching Byron and Adam's soccer game, but I'll leave my cell phone on so you can reach me at the number posted on the fridge. Jordan is sleeping — just check up on him every now and then, and call me if there's a problem." She pulled open the front door. Then she leaned in closer to Stacey and whispered, " 'Bye, and good luck with the persistent teacher."

Stacey smiled at this description of Vanessa. "Thanks. We'll be fine."

When her mother was gone, Vanessa took hold of Margo's wrist and pulled her toward the living room. "But you said I didn't have to be a student!" Margo objected.

"You're not going to be," Vanessa told her. "I've made you an assistant teacher."

"Oh." Margo seemed warily interested in this. "What does an assistant teacher do?"

Vanessa took hold of Margo's shoulders and pressed her down onto the couch beside eight-year-old Nicky. "An assistant teacher observes what a real teacher does so that someday she, or he, will be able to teach."

Jessi and Stacey stood by the stairs and exchanged skeptical glances. But Margo nodded and stayed seated. Vanessa squared her shoulders and cleared her throat. "Now, class," she began in a voice filled with teacherly authority, "today I will teach you about finding good subjects to write about."

"I want to write a poem about soccer," Nicky said.

Vanessa stopped to consider this, then shook her head. "No."

"Why not?"

"What rhymes with soccer?" Vanessa asked.

"Mock her," Jessi volunteered from the bottom of the stairs. Then she ran upstairs to check on Jordan, who was fast asleep.

"When Mallory plays soccer, the kids all mock her," Nicky suggested.

"They do not," Claire disagreed, scowling at Nicky.

"She's not a very good player," Margo said in the interest of accuracy.

"Yeah, but no one has ever mocked her," Claire insisted.

Stacey recalled Mallory complaining about some boys in her class who had given her a hard time about her athletic ability, or lack of it. She kept quiet, though. She didn't think bringing this up would serve any real purpose.

"All right," Nicky said, giving in. " 'I know a girl who plays soccer/When she does, the kids always mock her.' " He turned to Claire. "Okay?"

"That's better," Claire agreed.

"But now what?" Vanessa asked. "There's no place to go from there. Besides, soccer isn't a very poetic subject. It's not suitable for a poem."

"Wait a minute," Jessi spoke up as she returned to the kids on the couch. "In school I learned that you can write a poem about anything you want."

Nicky stuck out his tongue at Vanessa.

Vanessa's hands flew to her hips. "Who is the teacher around here?" she demanded. "I'm teaching poetry my way." She turned to Nicky with a stern expression. "I saw that tongue, young man. You are on detention."

"Oh, yeah? What are you going to do to me?"

Vanessa strode up to him and snatched an electronic game from his shirt pocket. "I will keep this until your detention is over," she informed him.

Nicky leaped up from the couch. "Give me that!" He tried to grab it. Vanessa held it behind her back. Then she knelt and shot it across the floor, sending it spinning under the couch.

"Vanessa!" Nicky shouted indignantly. He dropped to his stomach and tried to fish it out. "I can't reach it!"

Vanessa grinned. "You'll have to wait until one of the triplets comes home to help you move the couch." She peered at Margo and Claire. "See what happens when you act up in my class?"

"But I'm a teacher," Margo reminded her.

"A *student* teacher."

"You said *assistant* teacher."

"It's the same thing," Vanessa replied. "Now, if we might get back to class, please."

"I'm not playing," Nicky announced.

"Nicky, I think you *are* playing," Vanessa said confidently. "Because if you aren't, I can report on a certain someone and his friends who stomped all over the bushes by the driveway the other day while trying to catch a ball. Right now, Mom and Dad think Pow did it." (Pow is the Pikes' basset hound.) "But I know what really happened."

"It was an accident!" Nicky cried.

"You can discuss that with Mom and Dad. You know they told you to play ball in the backyard, not the front."

"It's not nice to tattle," Claire said. "I won't play either if you tell on Nicky."

Vanessa's hand went to her forehead. "I just

thought of another poem. 'I know a girl named Claire, who hates to brush her hair/So, what she did, the brush she hid. But I could tell her mother where.' "

"I didn't hide it," Claire protested.

"I know. You threw it in the garbage, which is even worse."

Stacey stepped into the living room. "Vanessa, you can't blackmail them into being your students. This was supposed to be fun."

"No, it wasn't. It was to teach poetry. It's serious."

"But I can't even write yet!" Claire cried.

Vanessa folded her arms and studied her students. "You know, I've noticed that Margo and Nicky don't write very well either."

"I write fine," Margo said.

"Not really," Vanessa disagreed. "Your handwriting isn't the greatest."

She took some white paper from the coffee table and handed them each a sheet. "Take out your pencils. We're going to go over basic letter formation. We will begin by making capital *A*'s. I want twenty of them on your papers."

Claire was interested in this. "I make very good *A*'s," she said.

"I'm not doing this anymore," Margo shouted, slamming down her pencil.

"Fine," Vanessa said. "But Mom and Dad will be so disappointed in you when they hear how you were scolded today for blowing straw wrappers in the lunchroom."

"I didn't start it," Margo said sulkily. She went back to making Λ's.

"Should we stop this?" Jessi asked Stacey. "It doesn't seem right. It's as if they're her prisoners."

Stacey sighed. "But what if Vanessa really tells on them?" Stacey asked to see Vanessa alone in the kitchen. "You wouldn't really tattle on them, would you?" she asked.

"Maybe I would, maybe I wouldn't."

"You can't force them to play," Stacey insisted.

"Oh, they really want to learn poetry," Vanessa assured her. "You just have to know how to control the class if you're going to be a teacher."

"*Your* teachers don't threaten to tell on you if you don't obey the rules. They don't blackmail you."

"Of course they do. They say, 'I'll report you to the principal.' Or, 'Your parents will be getting a note about this.' It's exactly what they do. Where do you think I got the idea from?"

Stacey was stunned. She didn't know how to argue with this.

"Excuse me, but I have to get back to class," Vanessa told her.

Jessi poked her head in the kitchen door.

"Did you get through to her?" she asked.

Stacey shook her head. "Not even a little."

Jessi looked out into the living room, where class was continuing. "What are we going to do?"

"I don't know, but we have to do something. Nicky, Margo, and Claire can't be held prisoners in The Vanessa School of Poetry forever."

CHAPTER 10

The TOT program was scheduled for a day on and then a day off. In other words, we taught only every other day. So on Tuesday, I was off.

I was surprised at how light and free I felt that morning as I opened my locker. I was a plain old student again and was glad not to have to think about Ms. Walden or Cary Retlin for a whole day.

Or so I thought.

Then I looked up from my books and saw Ms. Walden striding purposefully down the hall, her sights locked onto a definite target. Me.

"Thomas, I need to talk to you," she said. "When will you have a minute today?"

"Ummm . . ." I was so startled that I couldn't even think. "Before lunch?" I suggested.

"Fine," she confirmed. "See me in the phys. ed. office."

"Is everything all right?" I asked anxiously.

"We need to talk about some things."

If I had to wait until lunch to find out what this was about, I'd lose my mind. I certainly wouldn't be able to pay attention in my classes. "Is it about yesterday?" I asked.

"We'll talk later," Ms. Walden replied. "Hurry, or you'll be late for homeroom."

As she walked away, I made a decision. I didn't like Ms. Walden. I didn't know if she was different from last year. Maybe I had been different, younger, and didn't mind her gruff bossiness then. Whatever. I absolutely did not like her this year.

I knew Mallory had gone through a phase when she despised her. Then, when she joined the archery club, which Ms. Walden ran, she didn't loathe her as much. That was because she enjoyed archery and did well at it.

But all along I'd told Mallory that Ms. Walden wasn't so bad. I'd been wrong. I owed Mallory an apology.

I wondered how Mal was doing today. At the BSC meeting yesterday she'd been quiet — too quiet. I'd asked her how her conference with Mrs. Simon had gone.

"Okay," she'd replied. "She suggested I forget about teaching a story poem and teach a poem I really love instead. I'll choose something by Emily Dickinson. I'm not sure which one, though."

As you might imagine, all I thought about that morning was what my talk with Ms. Walden would be like. Was she angry that I'd lost control of the class? Was she about to fire me?

How humiliating would that be?

Thrown out of the TOT program!

I'd never live it down.

The BSC members would hear about it. Sure, they'd be nice. They were my friends, after all. But would they lose respect for me? Would they stop listening to the rules I made for the club? I imagined them showing up late, missing jobs, and not paying dues. The club would fall apart.

And what about Kristy's Krushers? Would the kids ever obey me again if they heard I was fired from TOT?

Calm down, Kristy, I told myself as I sat in math class. *That won't happen — none of it.*

For all I knew, Ms. Walden might have something good to tell me. Maybe Cary is the one being fired! Or at least transferred to another class. Now *that* would be great news.

I considered every wonderful possibility.

Cary had quit.

He'd been bumped from the program due to complete lack of seriousness.

He had been hit on the head with a soccer ball and was now wandering around somewhere with amnesia.

I didn't care why he might be gone, just as long as he was out of my way.

When I finally arrived at Ms. Walden's office, I found her sitting behind her desk. "Have a seat," she said, nodding at the chair across from her.

"I don't have your lesson plan from yesterday," she began. "Did you bring it?"

"I . . . I . . . didn't do one," I admitted. "I had one in my head, of course," I added quickly. "I didn't think gym teachers did them either."

"Why did you think that?" Ms. Walden asked, unsmiling.

"I don't know. It didn't seem to fit the subject," I answered.

"Perhaps if you'd done one, class would have gone more smoothly yesterday."

"Oh, I knew what I wanted to have happen," I assured her. "But you saw how Cary was. He ruined everything."

"Cary isn't my concern. You are."

She *had* to be joking! Wasn't she? Surely she'd seen how Cary undermined every attempt I'd made to run a normal class. She had to know he was impossible to work with.

"How am I supposed to work with him?" I demanded.

"Teachers have to learn to cooperate with one another, Thomas. We don't all like one another any more than you kids all like one another."

That was a stunning thought. I'd always thought of teachers as being this team of like-minded educators, moving through school as a single unit. If you ever complained, if you ever said, "Mrs. So-and-So is such a crab," to another teacher, that other teacher would always reply, "Mrs. So-and-So is an excellent teacher." The idea that they might disagree with one another, might not even like one another, was completely strange to me.

"How do teachers manage, then?" I asked.

"You have to give a little," Ms. Walden said. "Things can't always go exactly as you think they should. You have to allow other people to have input."

"Cary has no input," I pointed out. "His idea of student teaching is to let the kids run wild!"

"And what's your idea of how it should be?" she asked.

"Well . . ." Here was my chance to tell her how I thought she might improve her own teaching. "Kids should learn, but in a fun way. You don't have to yell at them and punish them all the time."

"I heard you do quite a bit of yelling yesterday," Ms. Walden said evenly.

"That was because Cary was making the kids crazy!" I cried. My voice was louder than I'd intended, but I couldn't believe that she was disagreeing with me. It was as if she hadn't even been there yesterday.

Ms. Walden leaned toward me. "Concentrate on what you want to accomplish. Write it down in a lesson plan. Go over it with Cary and get his input. Then the two of you need to make a combined plan."

"Cary and I have already talked," I said, referring to the decision we'd made to coach separate teams.

"That's good. Now get it in writing. If I don't receive any submissions from you, I can't sign off on the extra credit." She slid a paper across her desk toward me. "This is a class list. I thought it might be helpful in preparing for your next class."

I took the list. "Thank you."

She nodded, and I got the feeling the meeting was over. So I stood and left.

I headed to the lunchroom, highly annoyed. Ms. Walden had treated me as if *I* were the one who'd messed up yesterday.

But — okay — I'd meet her challenge, get the class under control, and Cary under control too. And it would all be submitted in writing, nice and tidy.

* * *

That evening, after supper, Sam and Charlie went to the high school for a meeting. Mom, Watson, and Nannie took Emily Michelle and David Michael with them to a friend's house.

Karen had a cold, so she stayed home with me. While she watched TV, I sat in my room, determined to write the greatest lesson plan of all time. Not only would I write the plan, but I'd add all sorts of additional lists for Ms. Walden.

I sat up in bed and began to divide the class into teams. That would eliminate a lot of confusion the next day. I didn't know the kids, so I couldn't divide them by ability or anything like that. I just split them up evenly.

Karen came in and flopped down on my bed. "What are you doing?" she asked.

"Planning my class for tomorrow," I said a little sharply. "It's really important, so you can't bug me. Okay?"

"I'm not bugging, I'm asking," Karen replied.

I softened. Karen's a good kid and I know she looks up to me. "I'm a student teacher and I have to write down everything I do," I explained more patiently.

"So what are you writing?"

"First, the warm-up exercises I have planned," I said. When I came home from school that afternoon, I'd watched all the work-out videos in the house, writing down the exercises I thought were the best. I was already planning a brand-new routine.

But I felt a little shaky about the exercises, not sure I knew them perfectly. Although I could do them with the tape, I wasn't positive I'd be able to teach them.

Then I had a brainstorm. I went over the exercises with Karen, making her do them with me. All the while, I watched my digital clock and noted exactly how long each one would take.

When we were done, I started my lesson plan. *New warm-up exercises — twelve minutes and ten seconds.*

How was that for planning?

I was sure my next class would be a big success.

Not even Cary Retlin could stop me.

CHAPTER 11

Only one part of my class preparation was left undone when I arrived at school that Wednesday. I hadn't gone over it with Cary as Ms. Walden had suggested.

I couldn't bear to.

He'd just make snide comments about my lesson plan, and I *really* wasn't in the mood for criticism, especially not from a jerk like him.

That morning, I couldn't stop admiring my lesson plan. I'd take a look at it every chance I got. Everything I'd written was so neatly presented. I'd retyped it on the computer. In my opinion, it was a masterpiece of organization.

I decided that even if I didn't require the BSC members to do a lesson plan, maybe I'd do one for myself. It really was a great tool for staying on track.

Armed with my lesson plan and feeling very optimistic, I headed for gym class. In the hallway outside class I met up with Cary. "Hello, Kristin," he said.

"Cary, we need to talk," I replied, trying to sound as businesslike as possible. "I've worked up a plan for today and — "

"Oh, so have I," he said, cutting me off. Reaching into the back pocket of his jeans, he produced a rumpled piece of lined paper. As he unfolded it, I saw his sloppy, smudged pencil writing. It looked as if he'd done this in two minutes, probably on the bus to school.

I took the paper from him, and without meaning to I must have wrinkled my nose in disgust.

Cary laughed. "It's not that revolting. I didn't blow my nose on it or anything."

Ewwww! I almost dropped the paper. Nothing would have pleased him more, though, so I ignored the comment and read.

Not that there was really much to read.

Have some fun. Give the kids a break from the usual torture of gym. Let them blow off some steam, hang loose. Play soccer like it should be played, nothing held back.

I looked up from the paper in disbelief. "You're not handing this in, are you?"

"Yeah."

"Aren't you worried about what Mr. De Young will say?"

84

"What's he going to do to me?" Cary scoffed. "I'm not even in his class."

"Don't you want the extra credit?"

"Give me a break. Like half a point is going to make any difference in my grades."

I put my lesson plan on top of my folder and showed it to him. "Well, luckily, I've worked out a very detailed lesson plan, so it really doesn't matter that you don't have one. We can follow mine."

He glanced at my plan for a moment, then leaned closer to me as if he were about to confide something. "Kristin, I think you'd better take a moment for a reality check."

"What do you mean?" I asked, annoyed.

"You are never going to get those kids to follow that. What do you think they are, little robots?"

"No, but Ms. Walden advised me to — "

He cut me off again, this time with a wave of his hand as he turned toward the boys' locker room. "See you inside. I'm out of here."

I drew in a deep, infuriated breath. He was possibly the most aggravating person I'd ever met.

Girls were beginning to head into the locker room, so I couldn't stand there any longer. I hurried in and changed into a clean white T-shirt and a pair of soccer Umbros, put on my whistle, and went out into the gym.

In one hand I had the phys. ed. boom box. In the other were three handouts I'd photocopied on Watson's home office copier. One handout was a list of all the new exercises we were going to be doing and a brief description of how to do each one. The second paper explained the rules of soccer. The third noted how the teams would be divided.

As the classes entered the gym, I handed each of the students the three sheets, which (with Karen's help) I'd stapled together.

Then Ms. Walden and Mr. De Young arrived. Like the last time, they hung back against the far wall, standing together. Today they were going to see a very different class than they had on Monday.

I loaded a tape into the boom box. Sam had lent it to me when he came home the night before. It was called *Jock Jam*, and it had only high-powered, super-energizing music on it.

Before turning it on, I blasted my whistle. It was great for getting immediate attention. "Hello, everyone," I said to the class. "You'll see on your first sheet that we're going to do a new warm-up."

"How can it be new if we did it on Monday?" a girl with heavy eyeliner objected.

"This is a *newer* new warm-up," I said with a smile. "You can follow me. If you get lost, refer to your sheet."

There was a low buzz of conversation as the kids glanced at their papers. "These are girls' exercises," a boy protested.

"What do you expect? She's a girl," Cary offered.

I ignored him. "No. They're basic warm-up exercises taken from the most up-to-date workout tapes," I said to the class, smiling at them. "Before I put on the music, let's do some neck rolls. Follow me. . . . And to the right . . ."

The kids didn't mind this. It was easy. "This is my kind of exercise," a girl said, and everyone laughed. I hoped Ms. Walden noticed. The class was more fun already.

After neck rolls, we turned to stretching, then to bending. I asked the class to do a light jog before I turned on *Jock Jam*. Now we were in for some heavy aerobics.

"All right, everybody!" I shouted over the pounding music. "Kick your legs out."

I didn't see much kicking.

So I demonstrated. "Like this, kick right, kick left." Although umbros are shorts, they're loose fitting and not ideal for kicking your legs up without revealing your underwear. It was a problem I hadn't considered until that exact moment.

I had to keep my kicks low, and I saw that the class was doing the same. "No, higher!" I told them.

"You're not kicking high," someone pointed out.

"Just kick!" I barked more forcefully than I intended to.

"Sheesh, what a grouch."

Luckily, I'd planned jumping jacks next. I could do those in my Umbros with no problem. As I jumped, I wondered what Cary was doing. From the corner of my eye I saw him doing jumping jacks in front of the class too.

Amazing. Was he actually cooperating?

I should have known better.

In a second I realized that everyone in the class was out of sync. They were bumping into one another and slapping hands as they jumped. Why were they so spastic? It took me only a second to realize: Half of them were following Cary, who was not jumping in time with me.

"Hold it!" I yelled as I hit the STOP button on the boom box. "Hold it!" I blasted my whistle.

The class stopped, breathless, and stared at me.

"What was that?" I asked Cary.

"Jumping jacks?" a girl offered.

"Not you!" I snapped at her. "I was asking him!"

Cary gave me a wide-eyed look, as if to say, *Surely you don't mean me?* "Jumping jacks?" he asked.

"You were completely off beat. You confused the whole class."

A seventh-grade boy called out, "You were the one off beat."

"Come to think of it, Kristin, you *are* sort of offbeat," Cary joked, which caused the class to laugh.

"Kristy, Cary," Ms. Walden interrupted, walking toward us. "This is going a bit long. Didn't you want to play soccer today?"

I checked my watch. Wow! The fifteen minutes were nearly up and the warm-up was just starting.

Ms. Walden's words launched a stampede toward the door as the class raced to the soccer field. A blast from my whistle stopped everyone in their tracks. "Walk!" I shouted. "And look at your team lists while you're walking. When you get outside, stand with your teammates."

Cary hurried after me. "You didn't put all the dweebs on my team, did you?" he asked.

"I don't even know which kids can play and which can't," I snapped. "And don't call them dweebs. That's just the kind of attitude that turns kids off to sports."

"I see," he said seriously. "You think screaming at them and blowing that whistle in their ears is the way to go."

"No! I don't blow it in their ears!"

He rubbed his ear. "Oh, you mean it's just *my* eardrum that's busted?"

"It gets their attention," I insisted stiffly.

Most of the kids had left the gym. I couldn't stand there letting Cary fire off his witticisms. Whether he knew it or not, we had a class to run.

I hurried out to the field, with Cary strolling casually behind me. I expected to see the kids standing with their teams, but they were scattered around in small groups. I blew my whistle and clapped my hands sharply. "Get into your teams!"

They didn't move.

A short, burly kid with a buzz cut pointed at another kid. "There is no way I will be on a team with *him*, he shouted, pointing. "He is my sworn enemy."

Sworn enemy?

The other kid sneered back.

"We're not having any of that," I scolded them. "You have to learn to work with your teammates."

"Yeah, like you and Retlin do," another boy called out. "Smooth teamwork."

Everyone laughed.

"This isn't fair," a girl whined. "You separated me from my best friend. I'm *always* with Jennifer."

Jennifer then stepped up to me. "That's

right. Ms. Walden always lets us be together."

"Everybody, forget those sheets and split into two teams," Cary told them. Before I could object, the kids were running around and — amazingly — in minutes were in two fairly even groups. Cary turned to me with a snide smile. "See? You just have to go with the flow, Kristin, and things work out."

"That's your team," I said, pointing to the right. "And this group will be mine."

I have to make a little confession here. It had only taken me seconds to size up the two groups in terms of athletic ability. And my kids were definitely bigger and more athletic looking.

There wasn't any chance I would let Cary's team win today. He wasn't going to show me up with his sloppy go-with-the-flow attitude.

"My team, over here!" I shouted. I was about to blast my whistle, but Cary had made me self-conscious about it. I waved to them instead.

"Okay, now," I said, after they'd assembled in a half circle around me. "We're going to win. Who here is a strong goalie?"

"Anson," a boy said.

"Yeah, Anson," a girl seconded. The other kids murmured agreement. They turned toward Anson, a large kid with white-blond hair, vivid blue eyes, and freckles.

After that, I made the decisions. I put the biggest kids in a defensive line in front of Anson. Assuming the kids with the longest legs were fastest, I positioned them closest to the kickoff line.

From the other side of the field, I heard Cary's team punching the air and chanting, "Win! Win! Win!" Did Cary know what he was doing?

I doubted it.

The kids took their positions on the field. I blew my whistle to begin the game. To my surprise, the teams seemed more evenly matched than I'd thought. Some of the small kids on Cary's team were fast.

And aggressive!

One skinny, wiry girl tripped a boy twice her size. I saw it clearly. She stuck out one bony leg and hooked it up under the back of his knee and dropped him. I wailed on my whistle. "Penalty!" I shouted.

Cary, full of attitude, barreled toward me, waving his arms. "Give it up!" he shouted. "Do you think a kid her size would intentionally try to knock a big guy like him down? You're seeing things! He tripped. Look at the size of her."

A girl from my team pointed accusingly at the skinny girl. "She's a green belt in karate. All the kids on that team go to the same karate school in Stamford. That's why they all wanted to be together."

My jaw dropped. Cary grinned at me. "You assigned the teams," he reminded me.

I lifted my jaw and put my hands to my hips. "Tell them this isn't karate class. It's soccer. If they try any rough stuff, they're in trouble."

"Ooooh, I'm so scared of you." Cary winced, pretending to tremble.

I huddled with my team. "If anyone roughs you up, just stop playing," I advised them.

"Those shrimps don't scare me," said a boy. "We'll show them. We'll make shrimp salad out of them."

My kids started punching the air, chanting, "Shrimp salad! Shrimp salad! Shrimp salad!"

The other team picked up the chant, changing it to "Wimp salad! Wimp salad!"

I blew my whistle to restart the game. The kids played hard. The ball flew, and kids batted it with their elbows and their knees.

Cary's team almost scored a goal, but Anson batted it back out with his head. He didn't seem to feel any pain either.

The ball was soon near our goal again and Cary's team gave Anson a run for it. One kid smashed into him. Sticking out his chest, Anson butted him back into one of his own teammates.

"Hey!" Cary shouted at me. "Tell your goalie to chill out!"

"He's a goalie, you jerk!" I shouted back. "He's doing his job!"

The boy who'd been knocked back by Anson jumped up again. Red-faced with anger, he smashed the ball toward Anson but kicked too high and connected with Anson's knee instead of the ball.

It looked intentional to me so I blew my whistle.

"Now what?" Cary cried angrily. "My team, disregard that stupid whistle!"

I grabbed his arm. "He kicked our goalie!" I yelled into his face.

I suddenly realized that something was happening off to my side. I jumped away from Cary and saw Anson punch the kid who had kicked him.

Other kids joined the fight. Girls began wrestling. Guys were hitting one another. There was some karate action going on.

I blasted and blasted my whistle.

Then a much deeper, louder whistle blared over mine. "Hold it!" a male voice boomed. Mr. De Young had appeared on the playing field.

His voice did the trick. Everyone stopped. "All of you! Back into the gym!" he bellowed.

Breathless and sweaty, the kids obeyed.

Mr. De Young whirled around to Cary and me. "What started this free-for-all?" he demanded.

"His team was made of karate kids," I announced.

"She's crazy!" Cary countered. "Her kids were all giants and they started pounding on my kids."

"That's a lie!" I shouted.

"Enough!" Mr. De Young cut us short. "You two are in *major* trouble."

CHAPTER 12

Mrs. Downey, the school secretary, gazed at me with disbelief. "Kristy, *you're* here to see Mr. Kingbridge?" Everyone knew that there was only one reason a kid was sent to see the assistant principal.

I felt like shouting, "You're right, Mrs. Downey. I'm a *good* kid and this is all a horrible mistake." Of course, I couldn't do that. For one thing, Mr. De Young was standing right there between Cary and me.

For another, I wasn't in a shouting mood. I was caught between two moods, in fact.

One was a killing mood. I wanted to kill Cary.

The other was a disappearing mood. I was so mortified, so humiliated, that I wished I could simply vanish.

Mr. Kingbridge stepped out of his office and, for a moment, studied us. "I can see you now," he said, beckoning us to come inside.

I felt cold all over. Physically cold.

Cary and I took the two wooden seats in front of Mr. Kingbridge's large desk. Mr. De Young sat in a green leather side chair. "I saw what happened," Mr. Kingbridge began. "I was coming in from lunch at the time. It was quite a display."

Cary and I exchanged a darting, guilty glance.

"What do you two have to say for yourselves?" he asked.

Somehow, this didn't seem like the time nor the place to start accusing Cary. This was the assistant principal, after all.

Cary didn't accuse me of anything either.

Not that he would have had much to say. But the way his twisted mind worked, he probably could have come up with something if he tried.

"Things just got out of hand," I said quietly, feeling that Mr. Kingbridge expected one of us to say something.

"And why was that?" he demanded.

Again, Cary and I looked at each other. It was as if we were searching each other for silent clues as to how to answer. Now that we were in deep trouble, we were finally working together.

"I suppose we got the kids a little too worked up," Cary admitted. "And we got mad at each other, so they took their cue from us."

I was shocked. And, in a way, impressed. He was more honest than I'd been able to be. I knew he was right. We'd both been so competitive that we'd whipped the kids into a kind of war mode.

Mr. Kingbridge slapped his desk with angry impatience. My heart was pounding as he went on. "Did the two of you think stirring these kids into a frenzy was a good idea? We currently have a seventh-grade girl in the nurse's office with a black eye. A boy is being rushed to his dentist with his missing tooth in a jar filled with milk. We've sent another girl to the hospital with a possible broken arm. Was this what you wanted to accomplish?"

"No, sir," I mumbled.

"No," Cary agreed.

"Then, what did you think was going to happen?"

"I guess we each just wanted to win," I said in a voice so low that Mr. Kingbridge made me repeat myself. "We each wanted to win."

"Are you two the kind of future teachers we can expect? I certainly hope not," Mr. Kingbridge continued. "You have obviously not learned anything from the TOT program so far. If this is the behavior of our TOT volunteers, you can bet we won't repeat the program next year. I will give you one more chance. Your next class had better be taught *perfectly*."

I felt so guilty. They might cancel the TOT program because of something I'd done. I was used to hearing about other kids messing up like this — but not me.

I was waiting for some kind of punishment to follow. Mr. Kingbridge just cast a disgusted look at us, waved his hand, and said, "You can go." He asked Mr. De Young to stay behind. "I think you can kiss that extra credit good-bye," Cary commented as we walked out of the office.

I nodded. He was probably right.

Then, to my amazement, he began to laugh.

"What's so funny?" I demanded.

"You thought you were giving me the geeks and they turned out to be karate commandos." He laughed, falling against the tiled wall.

I was too shaken to find any humor in the situation. I left him there, laughing like an idiot.

We'd spent so much time waiting for Mr. Kingbridge to see us, that I'd missed my entire lunch period and the beginning of English.

Class was in full session as I slipped through the back door and into my seat. I had forgotten that Mallory would be teaching.

She stood in front of the class, looking as pale and miserable as she had on Monday. "I'd like to recite one of my favorite poems by Emily Dickinson, one of my favorite poets," she said in a voice so small I could hardly hear her.

"Talk louder!" Lane Reynolds shouted.

Mallory cleared her throat and raised her voice a little, but not enough to make a strong improvement. " 'I'm Nobody! Who Are You?' by Emily Dickinson," she said shakily. " 'I'm nobody! Who are you?/ Are you nobody, too? / Then there's a pair of us — don't tell! / They'd banish us, you know.' "

"That's pretty stupid," Cokie said.

"Cokie!" Mrs. Simon scolded sharply from her seat in the back of the class.

"It might seem silly when you first read it," Mallory said, "but Emily Dickinson wasn't stupid or silly."

"No, she was a nobody — like Spaz Girl," Shane said in a too-loud whisper.

Mrs. Simon stood up abruptly. "If I hear one more rude comment from this class, you will all have an extra report to do."

I caught Mary Anne's eye. She shook her head sadly and rolled her eyes.

"Does anyone have any thoughts on this poem?" Mallory asked. I didn't have a single thought. I could barely think at all after what I'd just been through. But no one else was responding and Mallory looked as though she might cry, so I shot up my hand.

"Yes, Kristy," she said with a grateful half smile.

"I think everyone feels like a nobody sometimes," I ventured. "But wasn't she a famous poet? Why should she feel that way?"

"She wasn't as famous in her lifetime as she is today," Mallory answered. "In fact, she lived a very quiet, secluded life in the country. She never married or had children."

Parker raised his hand and Mallory called on him. Parker has a definite obnoxious side, so I felt nervous. "So, what you're saying, then," he began, "is that Emily Dickinson was a Spaz Girl, much like yourself. Is that correct?"

Mallory froze. She was too nervous to think of a snappy comeback.

And I was too angry to keep quiet.

"No, dirt-for-brains!" I shouted. "She means Emily Dickinson couldn't deal with living in a world full of morons like you!"

Parker was about to reply nastily, but Mrs. Simon spoke first. "That's it! You will all write a ten-page report on Emily Dickinson, due next week."

"That's no fair!" Cokie whined.

I looked to the front, wondering how Mallory was taking all this. I was just in time to see her tearstained face as she walked out the door.

CHAPTER 13

"What a rotten day you guys have had," Mary Anne said sympathetically that afternoon. She was walking home from school with Mallory and me. I was going to spend the afternoon with her. Everyone else had gone directly off to sitting jobs.

Mary Anne was the only one of the three of us who was in a decent mood.

"Everyone in the entire school is now calling me Spaz Girl," Mallory stated dully.

"Not *everyone*," Mary Anne protested.

"Practically," Mallory insisted. "Some sixth-grade boys called me that name. How would they know about it if it wasn't all over school?"

I wanted to say something helpful, but she was right. It was all over school. I'd heard it myself. I don't think most of the kids meant to be really hurtful. They just thought it was funny and never stopped to consider how it would affect Mallory.

102

"The program should be called ROT instead of TOT," Mallory grumbled. "Because that's what it does. It rots."

"My class is going well," Mary Anne said. "I'm sorry it's not working out for you, Mal."

"Or me," I added. "It landed me in Mr. Kingbridge's office."

"You had the bad luck to have Cary as a partner," Mary Anne said.

"No," I disagreed. "It wasn't only him. I was as much to blame."

"I doubt it," Mary Anne replied.

Mary Anne is loyal to the end, which made me smile. For a second. "Thanks, but I was just as competitive a maniac out there as Cary was. I screamed at him and called him a jerk in front of everyone."

"He *is* a jerk," Mallory said.

"Yeah, but I shouldn't have said it in front of the class." I thought of how it had annoyed me that teachers rarely spoke ill of each other. Now I understood why they did it. It wasn't right to undermine the authority of someone else who was trying to run a class.

I understood a lot more about why teachers did some of the things they did. I certainly understood why they yelled. And I saw now that you had to be tough sometimes. There could never be any doubt about who was in command.

Which gave me an idea about Mallory. "You know, Mal," I said thoughtfully, "you're too nice to those kids. That's the problem."

"Too nice? How can you be too nice? Don't kids like it when you're nice?"

"Not always. I'm not nice whenever anyone is late for a BSC meeting."

"Yeah, but we understand," Mary Anne said. "That's how you are."

"How *am* I? Do you guys think I'm mean?"

"No," Mary Anne was quick to answer. "You're . . . you're . . . in charge."

"That's what I'm trying to say! Exactly! Mallory, if you act more in charge, the kids won't drive you nuts. You know how it is. Some substitute teachers come in and the kids go berserk. They know the teacher isn't really in charge. But other teachers come in and that craziness doesn't happen."

"I wonder why," Mary Anne said.

"Because they just take over like they've been there all along," I suggested, pretty sure I was right.

"How can I do that with a bunch of eighth-graders?" Mallory asked hopelessly.

"Half of them act like *first*-graders," I reminded her. "Go in on Friday and pretend that's what they are."

"But they're calling me Spaz Girl," Mallory cried.

"So? If they really were first-graders they'd be calling you Poo-poo-head. Would that upset you?"

Mallory laughed. "No. That would be too silly to bother me."

"It's no sillier than Spaz Girl."

Mallory didn't answer, but she seemed to be thinking about what I'd said. We'd reached the corner where Mal usually turned off. "We're going to work on our lesson plans before the BSC meeting," Mary Anne said to her. "Would you like to come over and work on yours with us?"

"Okay. I don't have to go home because I told Mom I might want to stay late to talk to Mrs. Simon again after school. After today, though, I don't think I can face her."

"I know," Mary Anne said. "Abby is sitting while your mom takes the triplets to soccer."

Leave it to Mary Anne to know this. As club secretary, she's probably aware of what half of Stoneybrook is doing at any given moment.

We continued on to Mary Anne's old farmhouse. It was quiet because her parents weren't home from work yet. We climbed the steep, narrow stairs to her room.

"Do you have any poetry books?" Mallory asked. "I had planned to do another poem by Emily Dickinson, but I don't think I should teach her again, not since I've turned her into

Emily 'Spaz Girl' Dickinson." She raised her eyes ceilingward, as if searching for the invisible spirit of the poet hovering there. "Sorry, Emily," she said.

"I'm sure Emily forgives you," Mary Anne said as she handed Mallory several poetry books from her shelf. "Although I'm not sure she forgives the kids in our class."

"Idiots," I muttered, flopping onto Mary Anne's bed.

Mary Anne took out her social studies books. Mallory began flipping through the poetry, and I put my hands behind my head and laid back on the bed. I had serious thinking to do. After that day's disaster, how could I plan a lesson that could work?

I couldn't take the chance that things would turn out the same way. And if they weren't the same, they would have to be . . . opposite. I sat up, knowing I was on to something.

The opposite of fierce competition was fierce cooperation. "A Passathon!" I said.

Mallory and Mary Anne both put their books down and stared at me. "What?" they asked in unison.

"A big game in which kids pass the soccer ball to one another. And if the kid you pass to misses the ball, he or she isn't out — you are," I explained as the idea took full form in my head.

"Cool!" Mallory said. "That encourages everyone to pass well. And it sounds like fun too."

Coming from Mallory, who hates gym most of the time, that was good to hear.

We spent the next hour and a half working on our lesson plans. I wrote up a plan — complete with a new, new, new, shortened, simplified warm-up.

"I'm going to teach this one!" Mallory announced. " 'Stopping by Woods on a Snowy Evening,' by Robert Frost."

"I love that poem," Mary Anne said. "But do you think it might be too serious for those kids?"

"I don't care. I'm already Spaz Girl. What have I got to lose?"

"Good for you," I said. And I meant each word.

CHAPTER 14

Wednesday

Students at The Vanessa School of Poetry were in full rebellion today. And it was too bad. If Vanessa weren't such a tyrant she could actually be a good teacher. Believe me, I found that out the hard way.

At the meeting that afternoon, Abby told us about her crazy sitting job at the Pikes'. "Oh, I'm so glad I wasn't there," Mallory said while the rest of us fell over laughing.

The moment Mrs. Pike left, Abby looked around the house to get an idea of where everyone was. After a few minutes, she found Claire, Margo, and Nicky lying on the floor playing a video game. "Where's Vanessa?" she asked.

"Don't know," Margo said. Something in Margo's amused expression made Abby suspicious.

"Nicky, do you know where Vanessa is?" she asked.

Nicky waited until Super Mario had bounced up three levels and been killed by a giant mushroom before answering, "Nope."

"*I* know," Claire sang with an impish grin.

Margo pushed Claire's knee harshly. "She doesn't know. She's just saying that."

"Claire?" Abby inquired, not believing Margo.

Claire drew her thumb and forefinger along her lips as if she were zipping her mouth shut. Margo nodded approvingly at her.

Abby wasn't sure how to deal with this. "I have to find Vanessa," she told the kids.

Bang! The big stuffed chair in the corner of

the room jumped. Abby jumped back. "What the heck was that?" She looked around for Pow, but he was lying by the stairs.

"Unh! Unh!" It was coming from behind the chair.

Abby flew across the room and yanked the chair aside. "Vanessa!" she cried.

Vanessa sat there with her right hand handcuffed to her right ankle and her left hand handcuffed to her left ankle. A gag was tied around her mouth. In seconds, Abby untied it. "You guys are dead!" Vanessa screeched at her sisters and brother.

Claire jumped to her feet. "She's loose!" she yelled. "Run for your lives!"

With the game still running, Margo and Nicky scrambled to their feet and tore up the stairs.

Abby sat on the floor next to red-faced Vanessa. "What happened?" she asked.

"Those little creeps! After Mom left, Nicky tricked me into trying on his plastic police handcuffs. He said he wanted to see if they still worked. Then Margo came around from behind and gagged me. They dragged me over here and put me behind this chair. Wait until I get them."

Abby tugged on the cuffs. "You need the key," Vanessa told her. "Nicky has it. At least I hope he does."

Abby dashed up the stairs. "Nicky!" she called as she rapped on his door. "Open up." The door opened a crack and Nicky peered out. "Give me the key," she demanded.

"I can't."

"Why not?"

"Because if you let Vanessa free, she'll beat me up."

"Worse than that," Margo said, stepping into the hall. "She'll make him go to her poetry school."

"She'll make all of us go," Claire added as she joined Margo and Abby. "We're going crazy!"

"Yeah, we're desperate," Nicky agreed. "She gives us homework and then yells if we don't do it."

"And she says that since I'm an assistant teacher I'm an advanced student and I have twice as much homework," said Margo. "Whenever I try to write a poem she says, 'Not bad, but I expect more from an advanced student.' "

"And I can't even write!" Claire added.

"Hey!" Vanessa bellowed from downstairs. "Let me out of here!"

Abby held out her hand to Nicky. "Give me the key and I'll talk to Vanessa for you."

Nicky dug in the pocket of his jeans and produced the key. "It won't help," he said as he dropped it into Abby's open palm. "She won't listen. She only talks — in rhyme!"

Abby headed back down and freed Vanessa from the handcuffs. Vanessa was about to charge up the stairs after her siblings, but Abby caught her wrist. "Vanessa, let's talk," she said. "They're only going to stay locked in their rooms anyway."

Vanessa folded her arms. "They'll have to come out sometime. And when they do . . ." She punched one hand into the palm of the other.

Abby guided her to the couch and sat down beside her. "Do you know why they did this to you?"

"Yes, because they're little creeps!" She hesitated and met Abby's steady gaze. "Little creeps who don't want to go to poetry school," she added more honestly.

"If they don't want to do it, maybe you should let them quit," Abby suggested.

"They can't quit. Nicky and Margo could be good poets. And Claire is learning how to write."

"It's not fun for them anymore," Abby explained. "You're too hard on them." Vanessa scowled at her. "Vanessa, who is the best teacher you've ever had?"

"Ms. James, in third grade."

"Why did you like her?"

Vanessa didn't have to stop to think. "She made learning fun and interesting!"

"Exactly! Why don't you teach me about writing poetry, but do it as if you were Ms. James."

Vanessa frowned. Then she smiled and asked Abby what she'd like to write about. "Soccer," Abby suggested.

"Nothing rhymes with 'soccer'!" Vanessa cried. "Except 'mock her,' which is dumb."

"Would Ms. James say that?" Abby asked.

"Probably not," Vanessa admitted. "She'd say to try it." She handed Abby a pen and paper from the coffee table. "So go ahead. Try."

Abby isn't much of a poet, but she gave it a shot. After about ten minutes, this was what she came up with: *When Lulu wants to play soccer/She takes her ball from her locker/When Ingrid tried to mock her/Lulu said she'd clock her.*"

She handed the paper to Vanessa. "You're right, 'soccer' is hard to rhyme," Abby conceded.

Vanessa read the poem. "Ms. James would say it was a good warm-up poem," she told Abby. "While you were writing, I was thinking. To write about soccer, you don't have to rhyme 'soccer.' I was thinking of something like — 'Running fast on the grass the soccer ball/I pass to a player close to the goal/I'm part of a team, part of a whole.' "

"That's good," Abby said, impressed.

"Not really," Vanessa told her. "It needs a lot of smoothing out. But you get the idea. A poem about soccer could be about something more than soccer. How it makes you feel, for instance."

"I feel great when I play soccer," Abby said. "I feel like an animal must feel when it's running at full tilt. No worries, no thoughts. Just motion."

"Can I try too?" Abby and Vanessa turned to see Margo standing on the stairs. She'd been listening. "It sounds like more fun the way you're explaining it to Abby."

"If you want to, okay," Vanessa replied.

Margo said she'd like to write about cats. "It's been done too many times," Vanessa said.

"Would Ms. James say that?" Abby reminded her.

"No," Vanessa replied. "Um, cats are fascinating," she said.

Margo smiled and got to work on her poem.

As Abby worked on hers, titled "Animal Grace," she noticed Claire had joined them and was quietly working on writing letters on the floor near them. Eventually, even Nicky came downstairs. He didn't say anything but stretched out in front of the TV with some paper and began working on a poem about the Super Mario Brothers.

"We all learned something," Abby said, concluding her story. "I'm even submitting 'Animal Grace' to the literary magazine." We all wanted to read it, but she insisted we wait until it was published.

I listened to the story and had the feeling that Abby, Vanessa, Margo, and Claire might not be the only ones who had learned something from the events of that afternoon.

It was possible that I'd learned something too.

CHAPTER 15

I called Cary after the meeting and ran the Passathon idea past him. I fully expected him to mock it. To my surprise, he didn't. Not totally.

"It's a little on the cheesy side," he said. "The kids might like it, though. And — after what happened today — if we try to start another soccer game they'll probably take out bows and arrows and shoot each other or something."

I couldn't help it. I laughed.

"Kristin, did I actually hear you laugh?" he asked.

"Maybe."

"Don't go getting all human on me," he teased. "I won't know what to do."

"You could try calling me Kristy," I suggested.

"Yeah, I suppose I could."

They don't think I'm the Idea Machine for nothing.

On Thursday, Cary and I sat down together at lunch and worked out exactly what we wanted to do. "How about I lead the warm-up?" he said. "It's not like they love your routines."

I was about to start arguing, but he was right. Why not let him give it a try? "Okay," I agreed. "Here's what I've scheduled." I handed him my lesson plan. "Maybe you'll find something helpful."

He read it over. "You're right, Kristy," he said. "There's some good stuff in here. Can I borrow *Jock Jam*?"

"Absolutely."

That Friday, the Passathon was a success. After Cary's warm-up, which went well, we began. There were no teams, so the rivalry didn't have a chance to heat up. Each kid passed to any other kid. Cary covered one half of the gym and I covered the other, both of us being refs for our own half only.

Ms. Walden and Mr. De Young watched us closely. I knew Cary and I were on big-time probation. Mr. Kingbridge even watched for awhile. I tried not to pay attention to them.

As the kids played, I kept Abby's story about Vanessa in mind. I didn't yell at kids for not passing correctly. I didn't call penalties for the slightest little nudges. As much as possible, I let the kids have fun.

"Well done," Mr. De Young commended us when the class ended. "I'd almost say you two have redeemed yourselves."

For a fleeting moment, Cary and I grinned at each other. Then we turned away.

"I had a dangerous thought," Ms. Walden said to us. "Would you two like to coach the kids for their big soccer game at the end of this unit? I'll pick the teams."

Cary and I looked at each other uncertainly. "It's okay by me." I spoke first. It would be a chance to prove — at least to myself — that I could be a responsible coach and not let Cary drive me nuts.

"Me too," Cary agreed. He stuck out his hand to shake mine. At first I was too surprised to take it. But as he was about to pull it back, I took hold of it.

"It's been an experience," I said as we shook hands.

"Definitely," he agreed.

I felt was so happy about the way class had gone that I hurried to English, sure that Mallory's last teaching experience would also go well. When I got there, Mallory was passing out copies of the Robert Frost poem.

"Oh, puh-lease," Cokie sneered. "This is about some old geezer standing in the woods

with his horse. Why doesn't he go home already?"

Mallory ignored her.

"Spaz Girl strikes again with another spaz-
tastic poem," Parker called out.

Mrs. Simon was right at his side. "Parker, if I
hear from you again, you'll be seeing Mr. Kingbridge," she told him with a calm fierceness.

Mallory's face reddened, but she kept going.
Indirectly, she addressed Cokie's comment.
"There's more to this poem than you might
think. In Robert Frost's poetry, the woods often
stand for death."

"Did he tell you that?" Shane asked.

"Shane!" Mrs. Simon warned.

"No, when I was researching the poem I discovered that many literary critics feel this is
true. As with all poetry, it's a matter of inter-
pretation," Mallory answered calmly.

Way to go! I cheered silently.

"All I'd like you to do while I'm reading this
is to consider the possibility that the narrator is
thinking about his own life — and his eventual
death — when he thinks about the woods,"
Mallory continued. "If you do, a deeper meaning of the poem might present itself."

"Or it might not," Cokie muttered.

A student from another class came to the
door with a note for Mrs. Simon. "I'll be right

back," she told the class, a hint of warning in her voice. "Continue, Mallory."

" 'Stopping by Woods on a Snowy Evening,' " Mallory began to read as Mrs. Simon walked out the door.

A wadded-up piece of paper flew past her ear. She put down her paper and gazed out over the class, looking to see who'd thrown it.

"Grow up!" I yelled, although I didn't know who the culprit was either.

"Oh, big mommy has to protect her little baby?" Cokie taunted me.

"That's enough, class," Mallory warned, trying to take charge.

"Are you going to tell on us, Spaz Girl?" a kid named Justin sneered.

Mallory tried again. "No, but class isn't going to continue until I get some order."

"Fine with us." Parker put his legs up on his desk. After that the room became chaotic. Kids were talking and throwing things. Mallory stood in the front, helpless.

Mary Anne jumped to her feet. "Stop!" she shouted. Everyone froze. This was so unlike her that she'd stunned them into silence. "Please, show some respect," she pleaded with the class.

The class remained silent another minute.

Then havoc broke out again.

Mary Anne slid back into her seat, shaking

120

her head. Mallory sat behind Mrs. Simon's desk and read over her notes while spitballs, papers, and all sorts of odds and ends flew past her.

This was the scene Mrs. Simon returned to. Her presence — combined with the outraged expression on her face — snapped everyone back to attention. "You will all be writing an additional report on the poetry of Robert Frost," she said icily. She turned to Mallory. "Do you feel up to continuing?"

Mallory nodded. She came out from behind the desk and began her reading again.

She interpreted it dramatically, with a lot of feeling. I'd read the poem before, but it had never seemed so meaningful to me. When she was finished, I saw that Mary Anne had tears in her eyes. A few other kids did too.

Pete Black raised his hand. "So do you think the narrator really means he has promises to keep before he dies?" he asked.

"You could look at it that way," Mallory agreed.

Some other kids made intelligent comments too. When the class ended, some kids actually clapped.

Mary Anne and I rushed to Mallory. "You did it," Mary Anne said to her. "You were great."

Mallory didn't look happy, though. More

than anything, she seemed exhausted. "At least it's over," she said.

"But don't you feel great about how it ended?" I asked. "You really got their attention."

Mallory shrugged. "What? For ten minutes?"

A boy named Alex walked past the desk. "Nice job, Spaz Girl," he said as he went by.

Mallory grinned bitterly. "That's my new name."

"They'll forget all about it by next week," Mary Anne said.

I could have advised Mallory to laugh it off, but I knew that wouldn't be easy.

I thought of all the insulting names I'd heard kids call teachers. I suddenly wondered if that hurt their feelings too.

TOT had been a much more intense experience than I'd expected. Mallory and I would never be the same again. We'd learned things about ourselves and about our classmates that weren't simple to understand.

But one thing was for sure — I'd never again think teaching was an easy job.

Dear Reader,

In *Kristy in Charge*, Kristy discovers that being a good teacher is more difficult than she had expected. Over the years, I've had many wonderful teachers. My first favorite teacher was Mr. Mackey, who was my art teacher for first grade through fifth grade. (I named Karen Brewer's art teacher after him.) Mr. Mackey knew how to make art creative, fun, and interesting. (When he arrived at our class, he always raised his arms and swung himself through the doorway!) My next favorite teacher was Miss Kushel, who taught me in third grade. She helped give me a love of reading, and I adored her because she thought I could do *anything*. In seventh and eighth grade my wonderful creative writing teacher was Mr. Dougherty (whom Mallory's creative writing teacher is named for). He sparked our imaginations and told us we could all be great writers. There have been many other great teachers since, but Mr. Mackey, Miss Kushel, and Mr. Dougherty stand out. They gave me wonderful gifts and showed me what a great teacher can do.

Happy reading,

Ann M Martin

Ann M. Martin

About the Author

ANN MATTHEWS MARTIN was born on August 12, 1955. She grew up in Princeton, NJ, with her parents and her younger sister, Jane.

Although Ann used to be a teacher and then an editor of children's books, she's now a full-time writer. She gets ideas for her books from many different places. Some are based on personal experiences. Others are based on childhood memories and feelings. Many are written about contemporary problems or events.

All of Ann's characters, even the members of the Baby-sitters Club, are made up. (So is Stoneybrook.) But many of her characters are based on real people. Sometimes Ann names her characters after people she knows, other times she chooses names she likes.

In addition to the Baby-sitters Club books, Ann Martin has written many other books for children. Her favorite is *Ten Kids, No Pets* because she loves big families and she loves animals. Her favorite Baby-sitters Club book is *Kristy's Big Day*. (By the way, Kristy is her favorite baby-sitter!)

Ann M. Martin now lives in New York with her cats, Gussie, Woody, and Willy. Her hobbies are reading, sewing, and needlework — especially making clothes for children.

Notebook Pages

This Baby-sitters Club book belongs to _____.

I am _____ years old and in the _____

grade.

The name of my school is _____.

I got this BSC book from _____.

I started reading it on _____ and

finished reading it on _____.

The place where I read most of this book is _____.

My favorite part was when _____.

If I could change anything in the story, it might be the part when

_____

My favorite character in the Baby-sitters Club is _____.

The BSC member I am most like is _____

because _____.

If I could write a Baby-sitters Club book it would be about ____

_____

#122 Kristy in Charge

In *Kristy in Charge*, Kristy becomes a teacher for a few days — and finds out it's very hard work! If I were a teacher, I would want to teach _____.
One subject I would *not* want to teach is _____.
_____. Kristy is frustrated because she has to teach her classes with Cary Retlin. If I could choose anyone to teach with, I would choose _____
_____ because _____
_____. My favorite teacher is
_____. The things I like the most about this teacher's class are _____

_____

_____. If I could change anything about one of my classes, I would _____

_____.

KRISTY'S

Playing softball with some of my favorite sitting charges.

A gab-fest

Me, age 3. Already on the go.

S C R A P B O O K

ith mary Anne!

my family keeps growing!

David michael, me, and
Louie — the best dog ever.

Illustrations by Angelo Tillery

Read all the books
about **Kristy**
in the Baby-sitters Club series
by Ann M. Martin

Look for #123

CLAUDIA'S BIG PARTY

Something incredible had just occurred to me. And this weekend would be the perfect time for it. Mom and Dad hadn't said anything about not having friends over. Now if I could just convince Janine.

"Now that I've moved back to eighth grade, I don't have much time to spend with Joanna, Jeannie, Shira, and Josh," I began.

"I'm sure that's a problem," said Janine.

"And my BSC friends haven't had a real chance to mix with my seventh-grade friends," I continued.

Janine nodded.

"Mom and Dad didn't say anything about not having friends over, so I was thinking about inviting everybody here for awhile on Saturday night?" I made it sound like a question and crossed my fingers that Janine would say it was okay.

"Mom and Dad are certainly well acquainted with all of the BSC members. They don't know the seventh-grade contingent quite as well, although they've seemed pleased with your new friends," Janine said, staring at a spot above my head. "I don't see any harm in a simple gathering."

Yes! I was going to have my party.

Collect 'em all!

100 (and more)
Reasons to Stay Friends Forever!

More titles... ➧

The Baby-sitters Club titles continued...

❑ MG22877-3	#93	Mary Anne and the Memory Garden	$3.99
❑ MG22878-1	#94	Stacey McGill, Super Sitter	$3.99
❑ MG22879-X	#95	Kristy + Bart = ?	$3.99
❑ MG22880-3	#96	Abby's Lucky Thirteen	$3.99
❑ MG22881-1	#97	Claudia and the World's Cutest Baby	$3.99
❑ MG22882-X	#98	Dawn and Too Many Sitters	$3.99
❑ MG69205-4	#99	Stacey's Broken Heart	$3.99
❑ MG69206-2	#100	Kristy's Worst Idea	$3.99
❑ MG69207-0	#101	Claudia Kishi, Middle School Dropout	$3.99
❑ MG69208-9	#102	Mary Anne and the Little Princess	$3.99
❑ MG69209-7	#103	Happy Holidays, Jessi	$3.99
❑ MG69210-0	#104	Abby's Twin	$3.99
❑ MG69211-9	#105	Stacey the Math Whiz	$3.99
❑ MG69212-7	#106	Claudia, Queen of the Seventh Grade	$3.99
❑ MG69213-5	#107	Mind Your Own Business, Kristy!	$3.99
❑ MG69214-3	#108	Don't Give Up, Mallory	$3.99
❑ MG69215-1	#109	Mary Anne To the Rescue	$3.99
❑ MG05988-2	#110	Abby the Bad Sport	$3.99
❑ MG05989-0	#111	Stacey's Secret Friend	$3.99
❑ MG05990-4	#112	Kristy and the Sister War	$3.99
❑ MG05911-2	#113	Claudia Makes Up Her Mind	$3.99
❑ MG05911-2	#114	The Secret Life of Mary Anne Spier	$3.99
❑ MG05993-9	#115	Jessi's Big Break	$3.99
❑ MG05994-7	#116	Abby and the Worst Kid Ever	$3.99
❑ MG05995-5	#117	Claudia and the Terrible Truth	$3.99
❑ MG05996-3	#118	Kristy Thomas, Dog Trainer	$3.99
❑ MG05997-1	#119	Stacey's Ex-Boyfriend	$3.99
❑ MG05998-X	#120	Mary Anne and the Playground Fight	$3.99
❑ MG45575-3		Logan's Story Special Edition Readers' Request	$3.25
❑ MG47118-X		Logan Bruno, Boy Baby-sitter	
		Special Edition Readers' Request	$3.50
❑ MG47756-0		Shannon's Story Special Edition	$3.50
❑ MG47686-6		The Baby-sitters Club Guide to Baby-sitting	$3.25
❑ MG47314-X		The Baby-sitters Club Trivia and Puzzle Fun Book	$2.50
❑ MG48400-1		BSC Portrait Collection: Claudia's Book	$3.50
❑ MG22864-1		BSC Portrait Collection: Dawn's Book	$3.50
❑ MG69181-3		BSC Portrait Collection: Kristy's Book	$3.99
❑ MG22865-X		BSC Portrait Collection: Mary Anne's Book	$3.99
❑ MG48399-4		BSC Portrait Collection: Stacey's Book	$3.50
❑ MG92713-2		The Complete Guide to The Baby-sitters Club	$4.95
❑ MG47151-1		The Baby-sitters Club Chain Letter	$14.95
❑ MG48295-5		The Baby-sitters Club Secret Santa	$14.95
❑ MG45074-3		The Baby-sitters Club Notebook	$2.50
❑ MG44783-1		The Baby-sitters Club Postcard Book	$4.95

Available wherever you buy books...or use this order form.

- -

Scholastic Inc., P.O. Box 7502, 2931 E. McCarty Street, Jefferson City, MO 65102

Please send me the books I have checked above. I am enclosing $_____
(please add $2.00 to cover shipping and handling). Send check or money order—
no cash or C.O.D.s please.

Name _____ Birthdate _____

Address _____

City_____ State/Zip _____

BSC1297

THE BABY-SITTERS CLUB®

by Ann M. Martin

Collect and read these exciting BSC Super Specials, Mysteries, and Super Mysteries along with your favorite Baby-sitters Club books!

BSC Super Specials

BSC Mysteries

More titles ➡

The Baby-sitters Club books continued...

Available wherever you buy books...or use this order form.

Scholastic Inc., P.O. Box 7502, 2931 East McCarty Street, Jefferson City, MO 65102-7502

Please send me the books I have checked above. I am enclosing $ _____
(please add $2.00 to cover shipping and handling). Send check or money order
— no cash or C.O.D.s please.

Name_____Birthdate_____

Address _____

City_____State/Zip_____

Please allow four to six weeks for delivery. Offer good in the U.S. only. Sorry, mail orders are not
available to residents of Canada. Prices subject to change.   BSCM1297